THE MERCIFUL WOMEN

Also by Federico Andahazi

THE ANATOMIST

THE

MERCIFUL WOMEN

FEDERICO ANDAHAZI

Translated from the Spanish by Alberto Manguel

Doubleday

LONDON · NEW YORK · TORONTO · SYDNEY · AUCKLAND

The author and publishers are grateful for permission to reproduce illustrations: p. 9, the Villa Diodati, and p. 119, the Château de Chillon, from Edward Francis Finden, *Finden's Illustrations of the Life and Works of Lord Byron*, 1833–4, courtesy of Nottingham City Council Leisure and Community Services, Nottingham Central Library; p. 77, Henry Fuseli, 'Fuseli reading to the sisters Hess', 1778 © 1999 Kunsthaus Zurich; p. 141, 'Allegorical Figure of Erichtho': engraved frontispiece after Fuseli to William Seward, *Anecdotes of Some Distinguished Persons, Chiefly of the Present and Two Preceding Centuries*, 1795.

TRANSWORLD PUBLISHERS
61–63 Uxbridge Road, London W5 5SA
a division of The Random House Group Ltd

RANDOM HOUSE AUSTRALIA (PTY) LTD
20 Alfred Street, Milsons Point, Sydney,
New South Wales 2061, Australia

RANDOM HOUSE NEW ZEALAND (PTY) LTD
18 Poland Road, Glenfield, Auckland 10, New Zealand

RANDOM HOUSE (PTY) LTD
Endulini, 5A Jubilee Road, Parktown 2193, South Africa

Published 2000 by Doubleday
a division of Transworld Publishers Ltd

A catalogue record for this book is available from the British Library.
ISBN 0385 600534

1 3 5 7 9 10 8 6 4 2

Typeset in 12/17pt Erhardt by Falcon Oast Graphic Art

Printed in Great Britain by
Mackays of Chatham plc, Chatham, Kent

All biographies are a system of conjectures;
All critical evaluations
A bet against time.
Systems can be changed
And bets are often lost.

Julio Cortázar

PART I

There was something in the tone of this note which gave me great uneasiness. Its whole style differed materially from that of Legrand. What could he be dreaming of? What new crotchet possessed his excitable brain? What 'business of the highest importance' could he possibly have to transact? Jupiter's account of him boded no good.

Edgar Allan Poe, *The Gold-Bug*

I

THE CLOUDS WERE BLACK CATHEDRALS, TALL and Gothic, about to topple at any moment on to the city of Geneva. Further away, on the far slopes of the Savoyard Alps, the storm was angrily whipping up the wind, unsettling the calm of Lake Leman. Trapped between the sky and the mountains, like a hunted animal, the lake fought back, kicking like a horse, clawing like a tiger and lashing out with its tail like a dragon. In a hidden opening between the rocks that sunk into the waters lay a small beach: barely a strip of sand in the shape of a crescent moon, waning with the rising tide and waxing with the ebb. On that stormy July afternoon of 1816, a small boat docked at the western tip of the beach, at the head of the pier stranded like a ghostly skeleton overflown by gulls. The first to disembark was a lame man, trying to keep his balance so as not to fall into the lashing waters whose fury shook the pier's weak structure. Once his feet touched the ground, the traveller grabbed on to one of the piles and held out a hand to help his companions disembark: first two women and then another man. The group started to walk along the pier towards dry land like a troop of clumsy but cheerful tightrope walkers, without waiting for the third man who had been left to manage, not without difficulty, on his own. They walked in single file against the wind and up the slope until they arrived, sodden, merry and out of breath, at the Villa Diodati, the house on the top of a small cliff. The third man trotted along with short, quick steps, glum and not lifting his eyes, like a dog following his master's tracks. The women were Mary Wollstonecraft Godwin and her stepsister, Jane Clairmont. The former, in spite of being still unmarried, claimed the right to call herself Shelley, the surname of the man who was to be her husband; the latter, for reasons less well known, had renounced her given name and called herself Claire. The men were Lord Byron and Percy Bysshe Shelley. But none of these characters matters much in our story, except the man who disembarked last, and who was walking all on his own, far behind: John William Polidori, Lord Byron's obscure and despised secretary.

The events of that summer in the Villa Diodati are sufficiently well documented. Or at least some of them are. A stack of recently discovered letters may bring to light certain other events which have remained unknown until this day, concerning the life of Dr Polidori, the shadowy author of *The Vampyre*. And even more importantly, they may offer reasons for his tragic and early death.

As everyone knows, *The Vampyre* is the first vampire story, the cornerstone of the countless succession of stories that have made vampire lore a true literary genre which peaked (at least as far as celebrity is concerned) with Bram Stoker's all-too-famous Count Dracula. But no vampire story exists that does not owe a debt of gratitude to the satanic Dr Ruthwen fathered by John Polidori. However, the events that surround the birth of *The Vampyre* appear to be as mysterious as the tale itself. It is a truism to say that there is nothing as open to doubt as paternity, and yet this truth can be extended quite naturally to all literary offspring. Even though repeated cases of plagiarism (accusations old and new, whether proven or imaginary) seem to be part of the history of literature since its very beginnings, the controversy over *The Vampyre* did not stem from copyright claims. On the contrary, for some strange reason, no one wished to claim as his or her own creation the evil creature that was to break new literary ground. The novella was published in 1819 under the name of Lord Byron, but here a paradox must be noted: while Byron accepted responsibility for the doubtful 'pregnancy' (so to speak) of Claire Clairmont, he furiously and vehemently rejected all responsibility for *The Vampyre*, placing the blame entirely on the shoulders of his secretary,

John William Polidori. That is how the story was told.

And yet a tale as dark as *The Vampyre* could not, of course, have had a birth less murky than its contents. We know that, after Polidori's death, a considerable number of letters, legal documents and other writings were found in the doctor's possession, which were to contribute various undesirable facts to the biographies of several illustrious persons who had every right in the world to wish upon themselves an undisturbed posterity.

The correspondence in question is not new. Or rather, the absurd and scandalous controversies – juridical, scholarly and even political – to which these documents were subjected are well known to all. The arguments concerning their authenticity turned into something like a war. Expert opinions were published, as well as the results of calligraphy tests, ambiguous depositions of witnesses, and the indignant denials of those parties more or less implicated in the affair. But what was never, ever, made public was the contents of a single one of the letters, because – it was said – these perished in a fire that destroyed the archives of the court in 1824. All this was to be expected. But scandals, though giving the impression of being ubiquitous and everlasting, are often as fleeting as the time that separates one incident from the next, and they invariably end up buried under tons of paper and drowned in rivers of ink. The adamantine silence of all those involved, the progressive lack of interest of the public and, finally, the death of the main players relinquished into oblivion the controversial papers of which, it was said, nothing remained but ashes. The only document to survive was the no less dubious diary of John William Polidori.

As the reader will no doubt have guessed, an inevitable 'however' is forthcoming. Indeed, for entirely fortuitous reasons, some time ago I found myself in Copenhagen, where I was approached by a delightful character who introduced himself as the last of the teratologists, one of those commentators on ancient texts concerning monsters, a sort of archaeologist of horror, a researcher into whatever testimonies might have been left behind by the mythical 'terators' in their dreadful sojourn on Earth. In a word, my acquaintance was a taxonomist of unique and fearful human prodigies. He was a pale, thin man, with the elegance of another age. Ours was a brief conversation on a premature Danish winter night, in the Norden Café across from the Stork Fountain, at the end of Klareboderne Street. He told me that he was aware of a recent article of mine on a subject dear to his heart, and he had felt impelled to swap titbits of scholarly information with me. Since what I could offer him was not much, I was forced to confess that I was little more than an amateur in teratological matters. He seemed surprised that, as a native of South America, I had not heard the theory that much of John William Polidori's correspondence had ended up in an old Buenos Aires mansion that had once belonged to a certain aristocratic family with distant British roots. My colourful acquaintance had never been to Buenos Aires and the information he had was scant and imprecise. Nevertheless, with merely his vague description of the house and its location 'close to the House of Congress', I had no doubt about its identity. It was a dilapidated mansion which, through a curious coincidence, I knew well. Countless were the times I had crossed the threshold of this ancient house on Riobamba, whose vaguely Victorian architecture never fitted well with the features of Buenos Aires. I had always been surprised by the disproportionate palm tree that, in the very centre of the city, rose above its sinister garden walls, and by the wrought-iron fence, fierce and threatening, that guarded the patio, efficiently dissuading casual salesmen from venturing beyond the entrance.

As soon as I returned to Buenos Aires, I repeated our conversation to my friend and colleague, Juan Jacobo Bajarlía (surely our most knowledgeable scholar in the realm of Gothic literature), and he immediately offered to be my Charon on the infernal journey which began at the gates of the house on Riobamba. Let me say at once that, thanks to his wit as a lawyer and his wiles as a writer, we reached, after seemingly endless enquiries, our desired goal.

Having given my word to be discreet, I must not reveal any more details concerning the method by which we finally arrived at the alleged 'documents'. And if I protect myself behind the wary adjective 'alleged' and behind the cautious quotation marks of 'documents', I do it merely through a genuine uncertainty: though I cannot swear that these papers were apocryphal, nor can I affirm that they were not, because, to tell the truth, I never even had the opportunity to hold them in my hands.

During our meeting in the old house, I saw none of the original documents. Our host (whose identity I will not reveal) partly read out loud and partly glossed over the contents of numerous folders, consisting of practically illegible photocopies. The large dark basement in which we found ourselves could barely contain our amazement. Since we were not allowed to keep any material proof of these documents – neither a copy nor even a note – what follows is not a literal recollection but a laborious literary reconstruction of what we heard. The story that transpired from the succession of letters – fragments barely – is as fantastical as it is unexpected, suggesting that the facts concerning the origin of *The Vampyre* might lead to other incredible findings that would shed new light on the very notion of literary paternity.

As far as I am concerned, the possible apocryphal nature of this correspondence is unimportant. Literature (it is sometimes necessary to resort to a platitude) has no other value than to be literary. Whoever may have been the author of the reconstructed tale that follows – whether protagonist, direct or indirect witness, or mere narrator – I have no doubt that the whole thing is but an infamous invention concocted by a monstrous mind: a mind whose rightful place in the realm of the grotesque I leave to those more versed than I in teratology. Concerning therefore the truth (and, even more, the verisimilitude) of the events I am about to reveal, I must subscribe to the words of Mary Shelley in her preface to *Frankenstein*: 'I shall not be supposed as according the remotest degree of serious faith to such an imagination; yet, in assuming it as the basis of a work of fancy, I have not considered myself as merely weaving a series of supernatural terrors.'

Whatever the case may be, our story begins on the shores of Lake Leman in the European summer of 1816.

THE VILLA DIODATI WAS A SPLENDID THREE-storey *palazzo*. Along the front ran a succession of Doric columns above which rested a wide balcony protected by an awning. Three dormer windows, opening from the attic, pierced the pyramid-shaped roof. The servant, a man of few words, was waiting for the new arrivals under the protection of the balcony. With muddy feet, carrying their shoes in their hands, the four entered the hall and, before the servant was able to bring them towels, they had stripped off their clothes and stood stark naked on the marble floor. Mary Shelley, exhausted but happy, lay back in the armchair and, taking her husband's hand, pulled him towards her until he fell on top of her, and then wrapped her legs around his back.

Claire had taken her clothes off slowly and without a word. It was not, as Byron supposed, a gesture of blatant lasciviousness; on the contrary, she seemed absent, as if she were standing all alone in the small entrance hall. She sat on the arm of the chair while Lord Byron stared at her, enthralled. Claire's skin was of the same pale hue as porcelain and her profile resembled a cameo that had suddenly come to life. Her nipples were surprisingly large, crowned by pink aureoles that, even though contracted by the rain and the cold, seemed too large for Byron's mouth. Suddenly, Byron threw himself at her feet and, naked and panting, began to lick her wet skin. Claire did not push him away; she did not appear obviously to reject him. But noticing the icy indifference and the silence with which she met his caresses, Byron stood up, turned around and, perhaps in order to draw attention away from her obvious disdain, he placed an arm, naked as he was, around his servant's shoulder and whispered in his ear:

'My faithful Ham, I'm left with no alternative.'

The servant seemed more concerned with the mess in the hall (the clothes strewn all over the place, the upholstery soaking wet) than about his master's indecent joke and in any case Ham could never tell when Lord Byron was speaking in earnest.

At that very moment, John Polidori came in, untying the cape that covered his barely damp clothes. As he had taken the precaution of walking on the stone path, there was not the smallest speck of mud on his shoes. Faced with the debauched tableau, he made a grimace of puritanical distaste.

'Oh my dear Pollydolly, everyone is horrid to me. You've arrived just in time to fill my loneliness.'

John Polidori bore with stoic resignation the cruellest indignities from Byron, and he had learned to turn a deaf ear to his most heartless barbs, but there was nothing he hated more than being called Pollydolly by his lordship.

John William Polidori, who was then a very young man, looked even younger than he was. Perhaps his childish spirit lent him a babyish look that contrasted strongly with his adult traits. His thick black eyebrows appeared disproportionately severe compared to his innocent eyes. Just like a small child, he found it impossible to hide even the most basic feelings, such as distaste or excitement, sadness or joy, fascination or envy. Envy was the emotion he was least able to conceal. And the fit of prudery he suffered when faced with the naked group stemmed no doubt from the jealousy he felt of his lordship's new friends. Polidori eyed with suspicion all those who approached Lord Byron. His distrust, however, was not born of a desire to protect his lordship, but rather from an urge to keep a place for himself in Byron's fickle esteem. After all, was he not his lordship's right hand and did he not deserve recognition? John Polidori looked upon the foreign trio with a jaundiced eye, a look behind which simmered a boiling hatred, a malice both unpredictable and boundless.

To restore some semblance of order, with kind but firm paternal authority Ham clapped his hands, asking the guests to stand. As if they were a group of children, he led them to the rooms their host had previously assigned to them. Stark naked and still wet, they crossed the great hall, climbed the stairs and entered a long dark passageway lined with doors to the bedrooms. The stepsisters were to occupy the central chamber, which was the best appointed; Shelley was to have the room to the right, while Byron occupied the one to the left. Both the men's bedrooms had doors opening on to the women's chamber.

After Ham had shown each of the guests to their room, he noticed John Polidori standing a few steps behind him, in the darkest corner of the passageway. The servant approached Lord Byron's secretary and, eyeing him from head to toe, asked:

'Is the doctor expecting something?'

'My room.' Polidori hesitated, then offered the servant his small bag with a foolishly uncertain grin.

Ham merely nodded scornfully towards the stairs, and said laconically:

'Second door.'

Then he turned and left Polidori with his hand stretched out and the bag dangling in front of him.

Even though there existed between the two men a natural rivalry – the inevitable conflict between a servant and a secretary – Polidori did seem to inspire in everyone, even in those who met him for the first time, an insurmountable contempt, a feeling which Polidori himself appeared to cultivate. One could say that he felt a delicious pleasure in self-pity.

The small room in the attic was a dark hole barely aired by a tiny window that, like a watchful eye, bored through the tiles of the roof. It was exactly above Lord Byron's room, so that if his lordship required his secretary's services, all he needed to do was bang on the ceiling with a large stick that he kept for the sole purpose of forcing Polidori to run up and down the stairs.

John Polidori had just finished changing out of his slightly damp clothes when he noticed a letter on his desk. To be exact, it was some time before he realized that the object lying next to the candle was in fact a letter. It was a black envelope stamped on the back with an enormous red seal; in its centre was a baroque letter *L*. At first he thought that it must have been intended for Lord Byron and that Ham had left it there by mistake; however, when he read the white letters on the front, he saw that it was addressed to *Dr John W. Polidori*. There was no reason for him to receive any correspondence here, since no one knew of his arrival at the villa. And so, before opening the letter, Polidori ran downstairs to the pantry where Ham was instructing the cook on the tastes of his lordship and his guests.

'When did this letter arrive?' Polidori interrupted urgently.

The servant didn't blink. He barely emitted a sigh of annoyance.

'Apparently in Italy you don't knock before you enter,' he said, addressing himself to the cook, without even glancing at the young man. 'I don't know to what letter the doctor refers. Furthermore, the post is not my business but that of the secretary himself. However, I regret to inform the doctor that no letter has been delivered. And if any letters were to arrive, addressed to *me*, I would beg the doctor to let me know as soon as possible,' he added, without lifting his eyes from the cook's generous cleavage. And without further comment he continued his culinary instructions.

John Polidori returned to his room. He stared at the letter in bewilderment. The unusual black envelope seemed to him as inauspicious an omen as the appearance of a raven. If Ham had not delivered it, who else could have left it on his desk? Knowing he could expect nothing from his lordship's new friends except blind indifference, he was certain they would not have had the kindness to bring him his correspondence. Neither did it seem plausible that his lordship himself would act as his secretary's secretary and take a letter to his room. The most reasonable thing to do would be to open the envelope and read the letter, thereby clearing up this small mystery. But John Polidori was not blessed with the gift of pragmatism. When faced with the merest trifle, he would imagine all sorts of complicated scenarios and foresee the realization of his darkest forebodings. He could not accept the arbitrariness of life; on the contrary, he suffered from a compulsion to invest every little thing with a hidden meaning. He believed that the universe had been designed against his very person. He was gripped by the superstitious impulse not to open the envelope but to throw it into the fire. This letter could augur nothing but the blackest of fates.

It may be that, for the first and last time, he was not mistaken. It may be that John William Polidori's destiny would have been quite different had he never opened the threatening black envelope.

III

Geneva, July 15th, 1816

 Dr John Polidori

Sir,

Perhaps you will be surprised to receive this letter, or rather, to have this letter await you upon your arrival. I wished to be the first to greet you. Do not bother to jump to the end of this missive to discover the identity of its sender, because the truth is you do not know me. Nor do you suspect how well I know you. Before proceeding with this letter, I must beg you not to disclose to anyone its existence; my life depends upon your silence. I trust you to keep my secret from this moment on, now that you have read these first lines, since your life in turn depends irredeemably on mine. Pray do not read this as a threat; on the contrary, I offer myself as your guardian angel in this grisly place. Under other circumstances, I would advise you to leave immediately. But it is already too late. I have been here for barely a few months – against my will, I must add – and nothing good has come of this place, except your much-awaited visit. This summer has been dreadful beyond words; not a single day has the sun shown its face. I have never seen a place so desolate, so bare of life. Soon you will realize that even the birds have taken wing. I have begun to fear everything. Even my own person seems to me, at times, strange and terrifying – I (and I say it without conceit) who have never feared anything! However, very strange events have started to take place. Death reigns over the manor, and the lake has turned into a treacherous beast. Since the beginning of the summer it has pitilessly swallowed three ships of which not a timber has ever been found. They literally disappeared inside its black bowels and their crews have never been heard of again. Three days ago, two savagely mutilated bodies appeared at the foot of the mountains, near the Château de Chillon. I saw them myself. They were the bodies of two young men of approximately your age, who lived near the villa you now occupy. I don't know how they arrived, whether alive or already dead, on the opposite shore of Lake Leman. And what torments me most is that I cannot truthfully confirm that I did not have a hand in this sinister occurrence. I beg you, however, not to feel uneasy; I am jumping ahead of myself.

Your much-desired presence comforts me, not because I expect anything from you (at least not for now) but because the mere idea of protecting you (and there is no doubt that you will need protection) restores some of the courage I had lost.

If you lift your eyes, you will see outside your window the opposite shore of the lake. Now look at the faint faraway lights flickering on the top of the highest mountain. That is where I find myself at this very moment. As you read these lines, I shall be watching your window.

John Polidori stopped reading. The last sentence had left him shaken. He stood up, wiped the mist off the glass with the palm of his hand and looked through the window. Behind the curtain of water falling diagonally on the lake, he could barely discern on the far shore the mountains whose tips melted in the stormy sky. He could just make out two lights that shone feebly. He blew out the candles on his desk. Because of the storm, the room fell into almost total darkness. When he looked again through the window, he discovered that one of the lights on the other side was no longer burning. He stood watching in the gloom. After a while, he lit the candles again. And then, as if in response to his own gesture, the faraway light came to life once more. This first unusual dialogue filled him with terror. John Polidori was now dreadfully certain that someone was watching him.

I V

FROM THE FLOOR BELOW CAME THE MUFFLED laughs of Mary and Claire and the sickly smell of absinthe, tobacco and Turkish pot-pourri, a combination to which Polidori had never become accustomed and which provoked in him an irrepressible nausea. Without thinking, he opened the window but a superstitious fear forced him to close it immediately. Suddenly, the entire landscape beyond, crowned by the imposing snows of Mont Blanc, the entire panorama swathed in a translucent shroud of rain, was reduced to just that minuscule and watchful light which, like a distant Cyclopean eye, observed him from the mountaintop. As if moved by a will that was not his own, he returned to the letter.

I shall tell you about myself. I must, however, warn you that I shall have to reveal a secret for which you are perhaps not yet prepared. But I trust that, as you read this letter, your medical training will steel your enviable youth. You cannot imagine what it means to me that you should be reading these words. Nor do you have the slightest suspicion of the chains, as ancient as my long life, from which you are freeing me. Even though this may seem incredible, you are the first and the only man (beyond my family, if I can call them that) who is aware of my anonymous existence. But I have not yet introduced myself. My name is Annette Legrand. You are very young but, even so, perhaps I am not mistaken in assuming that you may once have heard speak of my sisters Babette and Colette.

Indeed, John Polidori had not only heard speak of the Legrand twins but, as far as he remembered, he had even met them once at the house of Miss Mardyn, or (he wasn't sure) perhaps at one of the scandalous parties thrown by a certain friend of his lordship, a Drury Lane actress. Yes, he remembered the Legrand sisters perfectly. John Polidori had been deeply surprised at the singularity of the (by then already retired) artistes. Not only were they identical, but everyone admired the incredible synchronization that seemed to govern their movements: they walked side by side and never stood more than a step away from each other; they laughed at the same things or showed themselves equally bored by this or that conversation; they shared the same inclination to interrupt the most interesting anecdotes just before the punchline; and they seemed animated by a single soul. But what had surprised him most was the undisguised lasciviousness with which they would scrutinize any man who happened to come near. They showed no shame in gluing their eyes on the most prominent crotches and following with their glance (sometimes even brazenly turning their heads) the path of any prospective beau. They would then whisper in each other's ear and burst out laughing excitedly, without attempting to hide their feverish emotions. They showed not the slightest inclination to deny the scandalous rumours about them – rumours that ranged from murmured gossip to indignities scrawled on the doors of public conveniences. Polidori even remembered having read in a newspaper the neologism 'Legrandesque' applied to a certain lady whose reputation was being placed in doubt. At least his lordship preserved a haughty dignity in the face of the rumours about his personal life, and took great care to keep up appearances in public. 'These calumnies are too vile to be answered with anything except scorn,' Polidori had heard him say recently, after an indignant gentleman had stopped him in the corridors of the Hôtel d'Angleterre, accusing his lordship and his 'pestilential friends' of being 'an incestuous society that offended the Crown of England'. In contrast to Byron, the Legrand sisters seemed to pay no heed to convention.

Polidori cast his mind back, his eyes lost in an uncertain

point far away in the distance. But even though he seemed not to see anything except the hazy landscape of his own memory, he nevertheless did not cease staring at the tiny light on top of the mountain. John Polidori dropped the letter on his desk. He paced back and forth, as if an explanation awaited him in a corner of his room. Suddenly he was seized by a thought. He leaned out of the window, his elbows on the sill and his chin on his fists, and spent some time scrutinizing, not the light on the mountaintop, but the faint strip of lights shining along the edge of the lake. He found it difficult to count them, but that very difficulty offered him a solution to his puzzle. A few of the lights on the shore died out, while others suddenly appeared in the distance; some sparkled feebly until they vanished, and some were probably nothing more than optical effects on the dark waters. He told himself that if, there and then, he decided to blow out his candles, at the very same instant one of those coastal lights would also surely disappear – and merely by chance.

He did not even have to blow out the candles; a fragile light on one of the rocks on the beach indeed suddenly stopped burning. He smiled. He laughed at his own foolishness. It was a hoax: his lordship must have been making fun of his superstitious imagination. To confirm his hypothesis, he doubled the odds. He wagered that if he now lit his candles again after blowing them out, another distant light would begin to shine in the darkness. And sure enough, after a few seconds he saw, somewhere in the west, a luminous dot. All this was obviously a stupid joke concocted by one of the two harpies downstairs. The laughter he could hear from below confirmed his conjectures. Now everything was clear: they had plotted this prank with Ham who had agreed to leave the letter in his room. That is why they had left him behind on the dock, hurrying on to arrive at the villa before him. Furthermore, he now remembered that at the Hôtel d'Angleterre in Geneva, on the night before their departure, the four friends had discussed several passages in that horrible book by Matthew Lewis, *The Monk*, and since Polidori had been unable to hide his unease they had amused themselves at his expense, telling more and more sinister stories. The letter he now held between his fingers had definitely been written by Mary or by Claire. Like the coastal lights that flickered and then went out with no fore-seeable logic, the light on top of the mountain (he said to himself) had stopped burning through mere chance. John Polidori folded the letter in four and prepared to go down-stairs and announce that the joke was over. But before leaving the room, to confirm his own stupidity and to con-vince himself of the weakness of the prank, he took the candlestick, lifted it up to the window and, using the envelope as a screen, placed it between the candle and the glass, hiding the flame for three identical intervals and then for a longer one. Having done this, he stared out across the water, and let out a loud guffaw at his own imbecility. But then, just as he was about to turn on his heels and leave the room, he saw with absolute clarity the light on the mountaintop cut out for three identical short intervals, and then once more for a longer one.

V

 FOR A MOMENT, JOHN POLIDORI CONSIDERED the possibility that he had lost his mind and that the inexplicable appearance of the letter which he held in his hands, the weird dialogue of lights, and the dark threats he was sure he had read were merely the fruit of a vivid hallucination. He asked himself what was the use of feeding the flames of his torment by continuing to read the sinister letter born from his own tortured reason (if indeed the ghastly piece of paper before his eyes had been spawned by his sudden lunacy). Of course, this explanation did nothing to calm him. On the contrary, the very idea of having become prey to madness increased his terror. So he returned to the letter in the hope of finding an answer that would reaffirm his sanity.

Let me warn you: have no illusions regarding my

38

beauty, especially with my sisters in mind. You are the
first to learn that the Legrands are not twins but
triplets. And there are many, many reasons for this fact
to be kept secret. Listen:

Perhaps I was the undeveloped twin of one of my
sisters, a monstrous excrescence grown under cover of
sibling flesh, one of those tumours that when extracted
presents the horrible aspect of an aborted human being:
a handful of hair, nails and teeth. You, in your pro-
fession, must have seen more than one just like me.

John Polidori lifted his eyes from the letter. His hands
were sweating and the paper rustled to the rhythm of his
trembling pulse. The words seemed to echo his thoughts.
Indeed, barely had he finished reading the words
'monstrous excrescence' when, against his will, his mind
threw up a memory of his student years. Now, try as he
might, he was unable to rid himself of the fearful image of
a certain jar inside which, floating in alcohol, was a hideous
lump, the size of a fist, which he had extracted from the
shoulder of an old woman. Polidori had always considered
himself a timorous hypochondriac, incapable of exercising
his profession with the strength of spirit that a doctor must
have; now this letter had come to remind him of his fear.
Like a haunting presence, once again he could see before
him the vaguely human form from whose fleshy middle
sprang a few teethlike bones, a sort of ancient foetus covered

in greying hair, the same hair as that of Miss Winona Orwell, the patient on whom he had operated. He could still see his teacher, the sinister Dr Green, holding the ex- crescence in the palm of his hand and, with an evil glint in his eye, repeating in a deep voice:

'Mr Polidori, give me your hand.'

Pale and on the verge of collapse, the young student had clasped his hands behind his back like a child.

'Mr Polidori,' Dr Green had said again with a calm smile, 'put out your hand or leave the room and never come back.'

Shutting his eyes and gathering as much strength as he could muster, Polidori had stretched out his hand and had immediately felt the viscous matter sliding over his palm like a worm.

'Mr Polidori, let me introduce you to Mr Orwell, your very first patient. I leave him in your capable hands,' Dr Green had said among the nervous titters of the other students.

Dr Green had turned and, addressing himself to the sick woman, lying faint in her bed, he had said in an officious tone:

'Miss Orwell, I'd like you to meet your younger brother.' The doctor had then pointed at the thing in Polidori's trembling hand.

Miss Orwell, an old woman with no family, living alone in a Liverpool poorhouse, had propped herself up on her elbows, peering at the object through rheumy eyes, and had asked innocently:

'Is it alive?'

Dr Green's rusty peal of laughter was echoed by that of his students. Polidori had felt the nausea rising in his gorge, before falling senseless to the ground.

VI

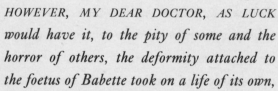*HOWEVER, MY DEAR DOCTOR, AS LUCK would have it, to the pity of some and the horror of others, the deformity attached to the foetus of Babette took on a life of its own, drew apart from her and finally became that which I am today. Dr Polidori, you cannot fail to recognize me, if not in what I am, then at least in the etymology of my condition. I am a teratoma – from the Greek teras, meaning 'monster'.*

I am indeed a monster – and I don't mean that metaphorically. I cannot even pretend to be included amongst those poor deformed creatures left by their parents at the doors of churches or orphanages. I suffer from a sort of chemical abnormality, from an unknown physiological quirk that has turned me into an amorphous freak. It is as if I were the residue from the formation of my sisters.

Animals, Dr Polidori, at least have the decency to kill their unhealthy offspring.

It was only to be expected that the malignant chemistry that shaped my physiognomy would also shape my soul in the image of the body it inhabited. Apart from my naturally coarse disposition, which is closer to that of a wild beast than a lady, I lack any attributes that might be described as delicate. The feverish emotions that in most mortals show themselves only secretly, in the dark, inhabit my spirit in a violent and uncontrollable manner. They surface suddenly and shamelessly, with no concern for social niceties: I behave according to my primitive impulses. In this, Dr Polidori, we may find we share a common trait. I am inexhaustible and lascivious, and I never measure the consequences of seeking that which I desire — or, rather, that which I need. I am nothing but one third of a monster that no imagination, either human or divine, could have conceived. I do not know what dark intelligence governs the course of nature, but you must not allow yourself to be deceived by the bucolic picture painted by pedestrian poets. Beauty is nothing more than the other side of decay and, in the end, invariably leads to death: the most beautiful flower sinks its roots in fetid compost. I do not intend to give you a humiliating description of my person; it is enough for you to imagine the most horrific creature you have ever set eyes on and then multiply its ugliness a hundredfold.

John Polidori did not need to hunt far back in his memory to recall the ugliest creature he had ever seen. As if his unknown correspondent were able to recall for him his vilest memories, Polidori immediately conjured up and was unable to dispel from his mind's eye one of the most atrocious moments of his brief existence. He remembered the abhorrent Abnormal Circus in whose sordid underground halls he had enjoyed the macabre privilege of witnessing a nightmarish parade of dwarfish figures, mountainous humps, nails like claws, hollow eye sockets, amputated and withered limbs, bestial grunts, mad laughter, muffled wails, heart-rending lamentations, mysterious sicknesses, giant probosces, pitiful pleas. Half wild and half subdued, some tamed by the whip and the leash, others rebellious in chains and fetters, the creatures moved along under the angry blows and brutal shouts of 'trainers' dressed in gold-trimmed livery. They advanced noisily in single file along the narrow and malodorous passageway that led to the cellars. Twenty-five freaks had been dragged from the four corners of the world, piled into the dank, rat-infested bowels of the sorriest ships and jailed in the underground warren of the Abnormal Circus. The intention was to exhibit them first, and then sell them off at public auction to the highest bidder. To strip them of any remaining traces of humanity, they had been made up and dressed in extravagant costumes. For the last compulsory lesson in pathology, Dr Green had assembled his class in these fetid cellars. According to the doctor, the forthcoming annual auction offered an incomparable living catalogue of monstrosities, a privileged encounter with the essence of pathos, which was impossible to grasp in everyday clinical practice. John Polidori remembered how, before the sale, Dr Green, with the 'scientific' complicity of the auctioneer, had tied to a bed a terrified little woman less than half a metre in height, whose eyes were dead white spheres that had never seen the light. To demonstrate that the patient was totally blind, he pulled out a match and lit it before her eyes. The woman did not flinch until the doctor touched the flame to her skin. Then, in an agony of pain, she emitted a guttural, muted cry that seemed to come from the depths of a bottomless abyss. Dr Green explained that although the patient was blind, she remained sensitive to touch. Taking up an ink-stained pen, he drove it into one of the fingers of the patient who arched her back in pain and stretched out a trembling left foot. Dr Green proceeded to describe the nervous system that joins the tip of the fingers to the toes, while the ink from the pen mingled with her blood. Shaking her head from side to side, the woman seemed to be asking what evil she had committed to deserve such punishment, as if conscious of the notions of sin and pity. By the look on her face, she appeared to be begging for mercy. Dr Green speculated out loud about the impressions the patient might be experiencing of what was happening – taking into account that she was blind, deaf and dumb – and advised his horrified students to reflect on this interesting question. At that moment came a deep cavernous voice, whose source could not be identified in the underground darkness, which asked:

'*What are the wordless mysteries that the dead try to communicate to us from the depths of the earth?*'

Dr Green turned his head and, seeing no one, took a few steps forward, a candle in his hand. Among the monsters, he made out the figure of a colossal man. He had the shape and hue of a mountain, a tiny head and a peaceful and infinitely sad expression. Tied to his ankle was a ball and chain.

Turning his back on the giant, Dr Green began to describe the so-called pathology of his previous subject when, suddenly, the giant stretched out an arm and with a single hand completely encircled Dr Green's head. The horrified students saw their teacher fly up into the air and crash down on to the stone floor. Dragging his ball and chain through the paralysed throng of students, the giant untied the little woman, took her up in his arms with the tenderness of a mother and, carefully stepping over the twitching body of Dr Green, was lost in the shadows.

VII

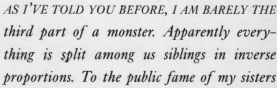AS I'VE TOLD YOU BEFORE, I AM BARELY THE third part of a monster. Apparently everything is split among us siblings in inverse proportions. To the public fame of my sisters I oppose my absolute anonymity. To their incomparable beauty I oppose my stupendous ugliness. To their frivolous stupidity I oppose (please don't take this as arrogance, since I do not consider this quality a virtue, on the contrary) my insufferable intelligence that hounds me and tortures me like a sickness. To their exasperating loquacity (on the verge of vulgarity, since they cannot resist the compulsion to interrupt those who are conversing with them) I oppose my obligatory silence. To their lack of scruples I oppose my inclination towards remorse, as if I am condemned to carry the weight of their atrocious crimes on my own conscience

(I am now obliged to make a confession, since I cannot plead innocence).

My dear doctor, you are the first to know of my existence. If you knew me and were to compare me to my sisters, perhaps you would be inclined to suppose that, like wealth, there exists in the universe a limited amount of beauty that, like everything else, is unjustly distributed. For every inch of my sisters' smooth, soft and perfumed skin, for each of their flawless pores, I can count upon my own surface the same number of chronic pustules and sebaceous cysts, blossoming boils and foul-smelling ulcers. For each of their wavy blond hairs, I can number half as many mousy wilted bristles growing from my tallowy scalp which is peppered with crusts of dead skin. From the moment we learned how to speak, they showed a tendency to do so in unison, a gift that would lead one to suppose that they shared a oneness of thought (to give a name to that which governs the movement of their tongues).

What I am about to reveal to you, perhaps the most scabrous detail of this whole confession, has no other purpose than that of protecting you. You will no doubt wonder, from whom? I shall answer: from my sisters and, consequently, from myself. Now the next question you will no doubt ask is, from what should you be protected?

My dear Dr Polidori, you must not suppose that my

*monstrosity is limited to my extreme ugliness. Not at all.
I know well your vast erudition. You are apprised of
the fact that there exist beings whose survival depends
on the appropriation of 'something' from their
brethren, even when this appropriation leads to
their victim's death. You are aware of the dark legend
of Countess Bathori who, it is said, needed her victims'
blood to preserve her youth. I imagine that knowing
that this was vital helped the Countess justify the
morbid pleasure she felt at seeing the blood flow from her
beautiful servants, and at the spectacle of death during
the inhuman torments to which she subjected them.*

*As it happens, my dear Dr Polidori, my own survival
(and consequently that of my sisters) depends on
obtaining 'something' which you possess. You have no
idea with what difficulty I must resist the temptation of
simply taking this 'something' from you because, I must
tell you, in only a short time, my sisters and I will suffer
agony for want of that 'something'.*

*I think it is prudent for me to conclude my confession
at this point, if only for the time being. I feel I have said
too much and I am exhausted. The summer will be long.
I bid you farewell and leave you with an entreaty: look
after yourself.*

Annette Legrand

On the verge of hysteria, John Polidori made a quick

inventory of all his possessions. His fortune consisted merely of the small savings he had been able to make on the salary that he punctually received from his lordship. He had no property: from his father he had inherited only the submissive character that irredeemably condemned him to the miserable fate of servitude. Like his father Gaetano Polidori, who had been the faithful secretary of the poet Vittorio Alfieri, John Polidori did not possess a literary gift: he could not expect the sweet dictation of the Muse, only that of his lordship's deep voice which, propelled by inspiration, seemed to run ever faster than Polidori's hand. What he did possess was a mindless and corrosive envy. How many times while transcribing the still unpublished works of Byron had he been overcome with the idea of plagiarizing his master!

What was that 'something' that Annette Legrand and her sisters wanted from him? He owned nothing, whether material or spiritual, that even the poorest of mortals did not also possess.

VIII

A GREYISH–YELLOW DAWN WAS RISING BEYOND Mont Blanc whose snowy tip vanished behind the morning clouds. Lake Leman lay stretched out like a vast empty plain. The faint sun gave off a cold light that mingled the uncertain autumnal colours: the pale red of the roofs with the pale green of the poplars, the grey of the rocks with the ochre of the sand. It was raining heavily. It had rained without pause throughout the night.

John Polidori woke from a brittle sleep, drifting back from that vague border that separates half-dreams from consciousness. He was crossing the threshold in which wishes materialize and reality is nothing but a blurred uncertainty. In this muddled mix of perceptions and intuitions, the secretary was nevertheless certain of two things. The first was that during the night, before falling asleep, he had written a story from beginning to end whose contents he no longer clearly remembered, even though he felt reassured by the evidence –he had only to open his eyes – of the manuscript lying on his desk. The second was that he had suffered a horrible nightmare concerning a letter whose macabre message he recalled all too well. A bad dream. Nothing more. And he felt pleased on both counts. He stretched his arms and arched his back. He scratched his head with well-deserved pleasure, and a faint smile appeared on his lips. He had written a perfect story. He remembered the discussion with his lordship a few days ago, during which he had insisted to Byron that there was no difference between the two of them. And he now recalled, with a little smile, his lordship's wounding reply:

'I can do three things that you'll never manage to do: swim across a river, shoot out a candle at twenty paces, and write a book that will sell fourteen thousand copies in one day.'

Polidori cared little for feats of physical prowess. But that the book he had just finished writing, barely a few hours ago, would outlive his lordship's fleeting fame, of that he was certain. The critics were not mistaken: Byron *was* a mediocre writer whose celebrity was due only to the scandals surrounding him. No, the marble pedestal of glory (the secretary said to himself) was made for men of the calibre of John William Polidori. The story he had just finished would sell not fourteen thousand copies but twenty-eight or even thirty thousand in a single day! Excited by this conviction, smiling happily, he woke up.

In the blink of an eye, John Polidori discovered his mistake, the delicious but ephemeral deceit with which dreams delude us.

Angry and frightened, he paced the room clutching Annette Legrand's letter, trying to forget its bleak contents; above all, trying to remember the plot of the story he had dreamt. But the harder he tried to grasp the strands of his tale, the faster they melted from his memory. For a moment, he thought he had rescued a paragraph, a brief trace of words that would set him on the right track. But after reaching for pen and paper, he found that his fragmented thoughts flew away like the dust of a shooting star. Nothing. The story he had dreamt had slipped like sand between his fingers. Nothing. Polidori sank into a renewed and inconsolable state of anguish. If the loss of a precious object or, even more terrible, that of a beloved friend was an irreparable tragedy, such losses could at least be partially replaced by mementoes, the stuff of nostalgia. But that which Polidori had just lost, that for which he longed most, left him with nothing, not even with the comfort of a single memory.

In this frame of mind he walked out of his room.

BYRON HAD WOKEN UP IN A VERY BAD MOOD. HE had a forbidding frown on his face. He didn't say a word when he passed his secretary in the hall. He didn't even answer Ham's greeting. He walked out on to the veranda and sat down to watch the rain. He breakfasted alone, his back to the dining room.

Polidori, furious at himself, was still trying to remember the story he had dreamt. He thought he had the glimmer of a memory, when suddenly, behind him, he heard a loud 'Good morning'. Graceful as a gazelle, Percy Shelley crossed the room to greet Byron. He pulled up a chair and sat down next to his friend. Polidori did not know what strange magnetism attracted his lordship to this uninhibited young man, whose manners and dress were so much more spontaneous and informal than Byron's protocol usually allowed. Under the same circumstances, and taking into account the mood in which his lordship had woken up, any other person who had dared interrupt his lordship's sulky brooding would have exposed himself to a stinging rebuff. However, Polidori could see how Byron's face broke into a smile as soon as Shelley began talking to him. Polidori hated the intruder with all the strength of his soul; his hatred was made worse by the fact that Shelley had interrupted the memory of the dream, just as it was about to resurface.

It was close to midday when Mary awoke. She was worried (as she told Shelley) about the health of Claire who had muttered in her sleep all night long, saying horrible things. Percy Shelley somehow seemed to know perfectly well what these things were; Mary said she wasn't going to repeat them but declared that she was not willing to continue sharing the room with her stepsister. She spoke in a whisper, as if she didn't want Byron to hear her. Polidori, standing by chance on the other side of the door, became an invisible witness to their conversation. Claire, said Mary, didn't want to get out of bed. She had not taken breakfast and refused to have lunch. Percy Shelley seemed more annoyed than worried. From time to time, and more frequently of late, he felt convinced that he had been mad to include Claire in their elopement.

Percy Shelley had plotted to run away with Mary, who was the daughter of his teacher William Godwin, and, since he would not admit that this act was a betrayal of his teacher's trust, he justified himself by being dismissive of his old master. According to Shelley, Godwin was no longer the man he had been: the heretical sage who had written the *Enquiry Concerning Political Justice*; the man who had spoken out against matrimony and even against common law marriage, which was why he had never lived under the same roof as the mother of his daughter. No, he was no longer that man but only his shadow: a husband twice married. The second time round, Godwin had married a harpy, the dreadful Mrs Clairmont, Claire's mother, a woman whose horizons stretched only as far as the narrow limits of her kitchen. How could he have offended in such a way the memory of his first wife, Mary Wollstonecraft? How could he have compared the fervent author of *A Vindication of the Rights of Woman* with this domestic scarecrow whose very existence was an affront to the female condition? No, Godwin was no longer the writer of fiery pamphlets proclaiming social change, but a poor scribbler dedicated now to children's stories and adolescent pap. Therefore, Shelley reasoned, to run away with the daughter of his teacher was not an act of treason; on the contrary, it was a way of resurrecting the ideas he had been taught and, in a sense, of vindicating Godwin's memory, of redeeming him from his present intellectual prostration. But what neither Mary nor he had foreseen was what a mistake it would be to include Claire in the long flight that had begun two years ago in Somers Town. They had left behind Dover, Calais and Paris and, after passing through Troyes,

Vendeuvre and Lucerne, they were no longer a trio of merry fugitives. Shelley, in spite of his eternally youthful appearance, was feeling old and depressed. Mary looked like a soul in pain. And Claire had become nothing but an inconvenience for the couple: she lacked all her stepfather's virtues but had inherited all Mrs Clairmont's malice. Claire was a disruptive companion: her fragile health and her unsteady mind (which she seemed at times to lose completely) had turned the journey into a nightmare and the planned sojourn at the Villa Diodati did not promise to turn out any more auspiciously. Byron, for his part, did not seem disposed to rid them of Claire. Although he appeared to enjoy her company, it was not to the point of seeking her constant companionship. In fact, Byron himself seemed to be quickly tiring of Claire. The charm of her beauty had begun to fade in the light of her moody character and, above all, of the intellectual poverty that he could now so clearly see resided in her soul. However much he might have wished to deceive himself, Byron could no longer deny that what had dazzled him in Claire Clairmont was the almost nymphomaniac sensuality that had now all but abandoned her.

They lunched in silence. For some strange reason, no one seemed the same after their arrival at the villa. Polidori could not help suspecting that something was being kept secret from him – even though this was a suspicion he was always inclined to harbour, under every circumstance and in every company. Perhaps he was merely attributing to the others his own deviousness, since Polidori himself was hiding something. And yet an impartial observer would have said that they were all hiding something from each other. The tense silence after the meal was interrupted by the arrival of a boat. From their places at the table they saw a small craft dock at the pier. The four friends could barely hide their unease. Polidori grew pale.

X

 HAM WENT OUT TO MEET THE VISITOR WHO was walking in the pouring rain up the path that led to the villa. After a few minutes, he reappeared in the dining room and announced:

'The prefect Michel Didier wishes a few words with his lordship.'

'Show him in,' Byron ordered with impatient curiosity.

Didier was a perfectly spherical man with red cheeks; the walk had made him slightly breathless and a whistle pierced his voice like the insistent call of a bird. First of all, the prefect wished to inform his lordship and his guests that they were most heartily welcome, and that he wished them a happy visit, even though the weather unfortunately, as they could see, was something of a disappointment. His was a long and verbose monologue. Even though he knew full well, he said, that the illustrious visitor was an excellent swimmer and oarsman, it was his duty to warn him of the danger of going on the lake in the present climatic conditions. He didn't wish to sound Homeric, but he was obliged to inform his lordship that three ships had recently disappeared into the bowels of the lake. All of a sudden he exchanged his serious expression for a smile and observed with amusement that he had learned of the scandal provoked by his lordship's presence at the Hôtel d'Angleterre, and that personally he was convinced that it had been a wise decision to settle at the Villa Diodati, source of inspiration for another poet whose name he could no longer remember but who would no doubt pale in comparison with the talented Byron whose book, he assured his lordship, he possessed (even though he could not remember its title) and whose verses he had been told were of unrivalled magnificence (even though he had to confess that he had not had time to read them). And yet he would not forgive himself if his lordship were to leave Geneva without signing the book that, to his shame, he had forgotten and left at home.

Byron realized that the prefect had entered a tangled web of words from which he could not find the way out, and that while he seemed to be trying hard not to arouse concern, his enigmatic introduction had indeed awakened their curiosity. Spurning the deluge of compliments, Byron interrupted the flustered prefect and kindly begged him to come to the point. There was nothing to worry about, the prefect said, but three days ago two brothers had mysteriously vanished. They were two fishermen, twenty-three and twenty-four years old, who lived not far from the villa. Nothing had been heard of them since and the odd thing about it was that they had not left in their boat, since it was still docked in front of their hut. If his lordship and his friends were to hear anything or see anything, he would be most grateful for their assistance. But he did not wish to unsettle them or to interrupt the peace and quiet of their sojourn. Therefore, having accomplished his mission, the prefect stood up, made his farewells, and even though no one showed the slightest inclination to accompany him to the door, he begged them not to disturb themselves since he knew the way out – until Ham thought it useful to explain that the door through which he was about to leave led in fact to the wine cellar.

It was at that moment that Polidori, his gaze lost far beyond the veranda, was heard muttering, pale and trembling, like a man in a trance:

'Somewhere in the vicinity of the Château de Chillon.'

He said this in a low but perfectly audible voice. The prefect froze on the threshold. Polidori had spoken with such certainty that it had sounded like a confession of murder. The prefect turned back.

'Pardon me?' he asked, trying to catch Polidori's eye.

With a start, Polidori realized that he had spoken and that, as usual, he had said far too much. It was too late to take back his words, but he could try to say something else, to complete the sentence with some trifle, to throw the prefect off the scent. However, if the bodies were indeed to be found in that very spot, as the letter had said, it would be clear not only that he had known where to find them but that he had tried to hide the fact from the police. For a moment, he thought of going to his room to fetch the letter and show it to the prefect, but a superstitious fear dissuaded him.

'Somewhere in the vicinity of the Château de Chillon,' he repeated, and added enigmatically, 'You see, I saw the birds fly in that direction.'

Percy Shelley took advantage of the fact that the prefect's glance had landed on him, to make a slight but meaningful gesture, closing his eyes, shaking his head and placing his index finger against his brow. The prefect nodded. The man who had uttered such a startling premonition did not seem to him to be in the pink of mental health.

'Fine,' he said, 'I shall consider your suggestion.'

As soon as the prefect had left John Polidori jumped up from his chair and pounced on Shelley, tearing at his throat.

'You miserable traitor, I saw that gesture!'

Shelley shook him off as easily as he would have rid himself of a fly, and grabbed him by the wrists. Byron interceded to defend his secretary, freeing him from the other poet's hands. This enraged Polidori even further. He felt like a child: he had not even managed to disturb

Shelley's smile and he took his lordship's defence as nothing but an act of mercy. Blind with rage, Polidori ran across the room, flung himself over the balustrade of the veranda and sailed out into the void.

XI

BYRON AND SHELLEY PEERED OVER THE balustrade and, in the pelting rain, saw the motionless body of Polidori lying in the grass. They ran downstairs as fast as they could. When they reached him, they saw that he was breathing, though with difficulty. He was also weeping bitterly, noisily, furiously. The thick bushes surrounding the house had broken his fall, and the deep mud in the garden had further cushioned him. All he had managed to do was twist an ankle. They lifted him under the arms and pulled him back into the house.

Polidori, leaning back in the armchair by the fire, somewhat bruised and covered with a blanket, suddenly felt deeply happy. Byron had made him tea and was sitting by his side, stroking his forehead. Shelley had apologized profusely and Mary was reading to him in a soft voice several pages from Rousseau's *La Nouvelle Héloïse*.

Polidori cast his mind back, savouring his recent feat of athleticism and, above all, his moral victory. Byron could never match such a show of physical daring. He savoured in advance the sweet, slow satisfaction of knowing that, at the right moment, he could toss like a dagger at his lordship:

'I can jump from any height without fear for my life.'

As foolish as it might seem, these were the petty fantasies that fed John William Polidori's pride. Paradoxically, they also showed his deep devotion to Byron, because on such occasions he behaved like a scorned bride. Another time, not long ago, he had tried to poison himself with cyanide, though the quantity he had taken would have been insufficient to kill even a mouse. But he felt that these extreme gestures raised him to the stature of his romantic heroes, since to be a martyr was as good as being a hero. He had heard Shelley say that the Western world needed to rebuild its idols 'with the dung of pity'. The phrase had seemed to him as true as it was illuminating. It reflected, after all, the story of his own life. And now, while everyone was offering him the concern and attention he deserved, he could not help but feel like another Christ, wounded, in pain, atoning, with all the faithful bowing at the bruised feet of Polidori the Redeemer. Furthermore, his little performance seemed to have restored his fading professional prestige: Byron had begged him to examine Claire as soon as he felt up to it, since he was seriously worried about her health. For the first time, he addressed his secretary as a doctor.

Close to nightfall and shortly before dinner, the tableau in the hall, reminiscent of a fresco of the Passion, was brusquely disrupted by the second appearance of Didier, the prefect. This time he seemed deeply preoccupied. Byron, with a show of displeasure, let him know that they had no news regarding the matter that concerned him; in fact, he said they had not even left the house since his last visit. He did not want the prefect to know about Polidori's brief adventure in the garden (he could imagine the comments that such news would arouse in England) so he made no effort to hide the fact that the prefect's presence was beginning to annoy him. But Prefect Didier was so absorbed in his own thoughts that he did not even notice Byron's abruptness.

'We found the two bodies outside the Château de Chillon,' he finally announced. His tone was solemn, very different from his previous chattiness.

All eyes fell on Polidori. Byron's secretary, leaning back in the armchair by the fire, merely raised his eyebrows, twisted his lips and nodded with a mixture of certainty and resignation, agreement and denial, as if to say: 'I knew it. It was obvious. It's a pity but why do you look so surprised?'

Polidori suddenly discovered that the ominous letter had a positive side. He had never felt so utterly important, a crucial and irreplaceable cog in the machinery of the world.

The prefect, full of admiration, observed Polidori by the light of the hearth. He begged him to forgive him for interrupting his meditation and asked him please to reveal how he had known the exact location of the bodies. Polidori sighed, closed his eyes and, after an enigmatic silence, at length deigned to speak. To tell the truth – how should he explain this? - it all stemmed from being half doctor and half poet. The practical instinct of the sawbones, coupled with the poet's ability to let his spirit soar, lent him what one might call a lyrical nose, a flair for the special scent of death, of seagulls in flight and of the treacherous currents of the lake. It was obvious, well, it couldn't be anywhere else, poor boys. He himself always refused to believe his own visions but, alas, the facts showed once again that he was right. Polidori lost himself in a convoluted and solemn monologue in which he lamented his unbearable cleverness and his insufferable gift of deduction, as well as his poetic sensibility. Why could he not be like the rest of humankind, a trifle less complex, a little bit – he did not wish to offend anyone by saying this – simpler? But what could he do? It was his nature and he must accept it with resignation. He spoke calmly and demurely, eyes fixed on the fire. Being wrapped in a blanket made him look like a sage from olden times. Shelley and Mary exchanged puzzled looks, which turned into astonishment and incredulity. They did not know Byron's secretary well, but enough to realize that he was incapable not only of clairvoyance but also of elementary logic. Claire, on the other hand, had not paid the slightest attention to Polidori's speech, and yet could not hide the tedium she felt listening to his gratingly monotonous voice; she felt as if all his babble would make her head burst, since she was suffering from a chronic headache.

'What will be, will be,' Polidori concluded mysteriously. Then he begged to be excused and retired to his room, with the weariness of a soothsayer after a visionary trance.

Prefect Didier let him go in respectful silence. Byron felt certain that his secretary was well and truly mad.

XII

POLIDORI RETURNED TO HIS ROOM absolutely convinced of the truth of what he had just said. Admittedly, he had obtained the information regarding the whereabouts of the bodies from the letter. And yet it was no less certain that he and no one else had, for unknown reasons, been chosen as the confidant of that mysterious spirit of the shadows. Unexpectedly, his fear had turned into a pleasurable thrill. He had the feeling that he might benefit further from the mysterious correspondence. He lit the candles and looked towards the mountains on the other side of the lake. The tiny light on the mountaintop shone once more. He smiled nervously and, with a touch of anxiety, looked down at his desk. Breathing heavily and with an agreeable sense of fear, he discovered, next to the candlestick, a new black envelope with the same red seal.

Dr Polidori,
What you did this afternoon was very stupid. It is a miracle that you survived. And I cannot but feel responsible. Perhaps in my previous letter I should have spoken to you about certain matters that would give you good reason to stay alive. I have told you already that there is 'something' that you possess that is of vital importance to me. And, if I may speak plainly, what I wish to do is propose a bargain, since I too possess something which, I know, is your heart's fondest desire. But to succeed, it is essential that we both stay alive and that we maintain the strictest confidence. What you said to the prefect could also have cost you your neck. My dear Dr Polidori, this is not a game. I no longer have any doubts concerning my own responsibility for the deaths of those two poor innocents. There are times when I fear I cannot continue to bear the weight of my remorse. But let me come to our business.

It is time for me to reveal what that 'something' is that I require to keep on living. Like water and air, I need the seed of life: the fluid that carries it through time, the vital substance that grants life to the dead through their offspring and holds within it not only the animal force of instinct but also the intangible lightness of the soul, the traits of our long-vanished ancestors and the character of those to come after we are gone; that which is written in the flesh of the first man and that which will also be written in the last, for ever and ever; the inheritance that condemns us to the end of our days to be that which we must be; the irrevocable legacy that grants us life itself, as firmly as it tears that same life from us in the end; that which carries in its sweet flow the germ of everything we are — I mean the essential fluid that only you men possess. You will have guessed, dear doctor, what substance I mean. Yes, doctor, I need that elixir of life much as any mortal needs food and drink. With the same mortal need that any one of you requires water in order not to perish, so I require that other vital fluid. I do not know for what monstrous reason the only substance that can keep me alive is precisely this one. Dr Polidori, can you imagine the terrible fate to which I am condemned? I have already told you that I am the most hideous being ever to have walked this earth. I need not add that I am not graced with the gift of seductiveness and that, on the contrary, the mere act of showing myself to a man — something I have fortunately never yet had to do — would provoke in him the deepest revulsion. You may ask how I have managed to procure this substance until now. You are an intelligent man: your imagination has probably told you how. I have also told you that my extreme ugliness is inversely proportionate to the beauty of my sisters. It is therefore superfluous to add that Babette and Colette, using their twin beauty, have supplied me with that which my monstrosity forbids me to obtain by myself. But I must tell you that if all their life they have taken upon themselves this (some might call it) unfortunate burden of assistance, they have not done so through sibling love or for the pleasure that such a task might entail. The truth is that, if it depended on my sisters' wishes, I would have been dead long ago. I will tell you the reason for Babette and Colette's 'humanitarian' support in due course. My sisters' reputation is well known. You yourself have probably heard the rumours about them: hussies, mantraps, strumpets, minxes, trollops, doxies, messalinas and even, plain and simply, whores are some of the epithets that have been hurled at them. Perhaps you have read with your own eyes some of these foul words written on the doors of public conveniences in Paris. There is little truth in these accusations. They are not naturally inclined to promiscuity. However, since they are obliged to perform this carnal task almost daily to obtain my elixir, I suppose they may have come to enjoy it. But that is an effect, not a cause.

Now that I have revealed to you what that 'something' is that you possess and I need, I must tell you the story of my family. I come from an old Protestant line. The strange turns of fate made my distant ancestors emigrate from France to England, and later, from England to America. My father, William Legrand, a man of precarious spiritual health, repeatedly threw away the inherited family fortune, and then built it up again. He was born in New Orleans and there he grew up with no other cares than those of a normal, wealthy young man.

When my grandfather died, my father became a victim of the most lethal plague ever to befall America — I mean the lust for gold — and spent his last dollar in the pursuit of this vain dream. With no other companion than his faithful servant (who always tried to help him keep a grip on reality), he settled on a lonely isle called Sullivan Island, close to Charleston, in South Carolina. God only knows how, two years later, he returned to New Orleans as one of the richest men in America. But his new fortune lasted no more than the brief interval that separates thunder from lightning: delighted with his good fortune, he invested all his capital in a senseless land speculation which almost cost him his life.

But with luck like that of Lazarus, my father miraculously rose again from direst poverty. Just when everything seemed to point to the end of the Legrand fortune, one morning there was a knock on the door. A laconic gentleman with a birdlike face introduced himself as a solicitor and informed him, that he, William Legrand, grandnephew of a certain André Paul Legrand, recently deceased in France, since there *were no direct descendants and no will, was the sole heir of the entire property of the deceased, viz. an un-assuming mansion in the heart of Paris including all the artwork, jewels and furniture and a sum of money sufficient to allow the three following generations to live in the lap of luxury.*

Now that nothing tied him any longer to the city of New Orleans (he had no family and his faithful servant Jupiter, who would never have abandoned him even under the worst circumstances, had died), my father decided to begin a new life in the land of his ancestors. His mind was made up as soon as he had signed the document read to him by the solicitor. The following month my father arrived in Paris and during the spring of 17.. he met Marguerite, the woman who was to be my mother and whom he married the following year. There is not much I can say about my mother because I never knew her. Shortly after their marriage – a year later, to be precise – my father's life became the stuff of nightmares.

I shall let the story tell itself: I will transcribe here a letter that my father sent to a certain doctor, in which, with bitter anguish, he recounts the beginning of my monstrous biography.

PART II

I

William Legrand's letter to Dr Frankenstein

 *Paris, March 15th, 1747*

My dearest Dr Frankenstein,

The words you are about to read are born from despair. I would have much preferred — taking into account the long years during which we have failed to be in touch — to speak to you of more pleasant matters. I must, however, confess that if I have kept silent over these past many months it has been because of this: the unfortunate course that my life has so unexpectedly taken. I beg you to help me, because I fear I lack the strength to continue to carry this burden. I need your scholarly advice and, above all, your noble discretion. Please take this letter as at the same time a confession, an attempt to expiate past sins and a request. Perhaps your medical wisdom will find for me a way out of the sinister maze into which, over the past three years, my life has been drawn. What I am about to tell you is the worst fate that could happen to any man. Don't think me mad; at least for now, I have not lost my mind. I pray God to give me the courage to send you this letter once it is finished, even though I'm afraid that shame will prevent me from doing so. In the last letter I wrote you, I gave you the happy news that Marguerite was pregnant. I remember with what joy I told you about the event, since it was long awaited and our dearest wish. Everything was going marvellously well and there was no reason to suppose that the outcome would not be auspicious. I know that you have since heard that my wife died giving birth because of certain unexpected complications, and I also know that you were informed of the fact that, even as her life was slowly ebbing away, with heroic selflessness and with her very last strength, she brought into the world beautiful twin girls. But that is only one part of the story. There are other events that no one knows and that I have never dared reveal because they are so awful and inexplicable that, in the grip of terror, I have not known how to proceed or from whom to seek assistance.

I shall try to tell you everything in as much detail as my shame shall permit.

During the frozen dawn of February 24th, 1744, seconds before a bolt of lightning was to announce the most awful storm of this century, Marguerite, whose confinement was drawing near, awoke with a start. I remember that I had spent the night watching her, I know not why, in the grip of an ineffable anguish that (I know today) was a sign of the dark events to come. I had the inexplicable certainty that something dreadful was to take place. Suddenly, as if mirroring my gloomy fears, my wife lifted her head from the pillows and, propped on her elbows, moaned as if she were to die of pain. She put her hand on her belly, as pregnant women do when they have the presentiment of imminent danger. Two things happened then in close succession, as if one led to the other. When my wife put her hand over her nightgown, I was gripped by the disturbing impression that her swollen belly was suddenly far larger than it had been when she had lain down a few hours ago; at the very same moment, the whole house shook to the sound of thunder. I tried to tell myself that it was an illusion, fruit of my sleeplessness. I lit the candles and, to my horror, saw that, indeed, my wife's seven-month bump, that until a few hours earlier had barely swelled out beyond her small bosom, was now a colossal abdomen. Little did I imagine that this was the beginning of a nightmare that would torment me to my dying day.

Outside the window the menacing sky closed over the world; the city was a distant and pitiful shadow, caught between the storm and the river. The Seine had never shown such fury: the waters had begun to beat the steps that lead up to the banks, reaching with monstrous claws the balustrades of the bridges.

And yet, had I been able to imagine the worst that might happen to a pregnant woman, my wildest fantasy would have failed to come close to what happened the night of the terrible storm. The rain was beating down furiously. With my palm I cleared the foggy window and saw how the curtain of hail and water was pounding the geraniums on the sill, while the cathedral beyond seemed to have become the very centre of the deluge, as if God's fury manifested itself through the maws of the gargoyles vomiting heavy columns of water.

I turned and looked with astonishment at my wife, whose face was now hidden behind the huge shape of her belly. She was screaming in pain. I went up to her and, in despair, wrapped her in the blankets and tried to carry her downstairs.

The coachhouse was flooded; the water was up to my knees. I laid my wife, who seemed to be at the point of death, on a discarded table.

The horses were neighing and stamping their feet, thick white steam issuing from their nostrils. It was almost impossible to harness them to the coach.

Marguerite was twisting in pain, and there was not much time left. I ran to the door and cried out for help, but no one came, as if all the inhabitants of Paris had been struck dead by a sudden curse. My wife's cry brought me back indoors. I saw her leaning against the wall, gasping for breath and covered in cold sweat, trying to stop with her hands a stream of blood gushing from between her legs. I felt faint, but somehow rallied my courage and rolled up my sleeves, ready to bring into the world the child from my wife's womb.

With a gasp, my wife, exhausted and pale from the loss of blood, made a superhuman effort. I introduced my hand and immediately felt the unmistakable shape of a diminutive head. I entrusted myself to the Almighty and pulled gently but firmly, until I saw the crown appear in the stream of blood. When it seemed as if, with just a little more effort, I would hold the small body in my hands, I noticed that something was blocking the exit. I turned my hand carefully and felt that there could be no mistake: next to the tiny head was another one of identical dimensions. Marguerite let out one last sigh and, to my despair, I saw that she had stopped breathing. With all the strength of my lungs I cried out for help, and, all on my own, God knows how, I brought the two infants into the world.

They were joined back to back by a horrendous pustule, a link of flesh that looked vaguely human.

Terrified, I saw this thing stirring by itself, contracting and dilating as if it were breathing. When I lifted the infants in my arms, they separated as if by magic, without my having to make the slightest effort. The thing between them fell to the flooded floor and floated away to a corner of the room. I tried to tell myself that its movements were involuntary, caused by the lapping of the water, yet something convinced me it had a life of its own. Indeed, when I leaned down to observe it, I saw that the strange being was actually trying to keep afloat. It looked like a small animal, somewhat like a tadpole, but its skin was grey like that of a bat. I could swear that the horrible creature was looking at me. Dr Frankenstein, imagine the scene: my dead wife lying on the table, my daughters in my arms, that freak looking at me with evil eyes and I, all alone, not knowing what to do. At once I was convinced that the cause of all my misfortunes was that sinister creature moving in the water. With my infant daughters in my arms, I held it down against the floor with my foot, to make sure it would drown. But then I noticed that my daughters were beginning to turn blue. They had stopped breathing, and I understood that my action against the one must be causing the suffering of the other two: because as soon as I lifted my foot, freeing the creature from drowning, my daughters were able to breathe again. The tiny monster now looked at me with eyes

*full of hatred. To my utter horror I saw it turn and,
quick as a rat, disappear through a crack in the wall.*

*My wife was dead. My daughters, whom I christened
Babette and Colette, grew up to be healthy and beautiful. The monster wanders through the underground
chambers and is rarely seen. She roams through the
basement library and the wine cellars, and I know of
her visitations because of her repulsive spoors. I have
seen her fight with rats over food. And even if I hadn't
seen her, I would know that she is alive because my
daughters are breathing. Many times, while trying to
fall asleep, I've suspected her ominous presence watching me in the dark, and I fear her heartless revenge. I
know she hates me. A wet-nurse fed the infants and, for
the past year, a governess has looked after their education. Today, the twins are strong and fit and their
identical beauty makes it difficult for me to tell one from
the other.*

The letter came to a halt halfway down the page. Polidori
turned it to make sure he had read it all. On the following
sheet, Annette Legrand took up the narrative again.

SINCE THE VERY IDEA OF A CONFESSION
*filled my father with shame, he decided not to
burden anyone with his terrible secret except
my sisters, and so the letter that he had begun
to write to his friend remained unfinished. I had to
rescue it from the wastepaper basket. Now you will
understand why my sisters have always made every
effort to keep me alive.*

*Dr Polidori, you may well imagine that my father's
confession had been touched by shame, and in spite of
his dramatic* mea culpa, *his story reveals only a partial
truth. I can't really blame him. However, even after
reading his impassioned testimony, I will never forgive
him his avowed intention to murder me. Nevertheless, I
speak the truth when I say that I am not unduly fond of
life. If I am still alive, it is hardly thanks to my*

father's love or that of my sisters. My childhood memories are engraved in stone. I do not accuse anyone of having condemned me to my virtual non-existence. None but my own reclusive self is responsible for my utter anonymity. Since my earliest days I have been irresistibly attracted to solitude and I have always felt the need (an almost physiological need) to dwell in seclusion in dark and silent places. I have learned almost everything from my rivals, the other creatures of the depths. From rats, a voracious appetite for books; from cockroaches, a keen observing eye; from spiders, patience; from bats, a sense of opportunity; from mice, the ability to cross vast distances through the very heart of darkness. I know Paris better than the proudest Parisian. I know all the passageways and corridors that traverse the city, on both banks of the Seine; and, if my interest lay in wealth, I could have stolen the treasures of Napoleon a thousand times over.

I have always felt a strong need to be close to my sisters. Perhaps because of our Siamese birth – our symbiotic communion which started in the womb. Because I was obliged to look after their well-being (after all, my life also depends on theirs) I was never able to lead a completely independent existence; it was as if we continued to be one single creature split into three. That is why, when we were still very young, while the governess, with infinite patience, worked hard at teaching my sisters the alphabet (they were never very bright — I might even go so far as to say they were idiots), I remained on the other side of the air duct, peering out from within the darkness. That is how I learned to read and write. That is also how I decided that my place in the house was underground, in my father's library and, beneath it, in the cellar where the wine was kept. My father had inherited a fabulous book collection from my ancestor, André Paul Legrand, whose passion for books had led him to collect more volumes than the first-floor library could possibly store. My father decided that these countless tomes were a veritable nuisance that took up far too much space and he ordered them to be transported, without any attempt at organization, to the bowels of the house.

It was a truly beautiful library. The pale light that descended through ground-level windows in soft and stately columns lent it a strangely holy aspect, as if it were a pagan basilica, a luxurious and Dionysian temple that, abandoned and in ruins, offered itself to me, and to me alone, as the most tempting of sins. The room was filled with the sweet aroma of damp paper and leather bindings, and the books, with their edges gnawed by rats, their pages drilled by bookworms and the destruction wrought by mould, looked like dead animals on which innumerable underground creatures fed. (This serves us as a reminder, Dr Polidori, that whoever writes with an eye on posthumous fame is headed in the wrong direction.) And in the midst of all this feasting, scavenger that I am, I also sought my share. Mine was a long and ruthless fight against the rats that seemed intent on devouring the very books I was keeping for my own consumption. It was an unequal fight, since I was all alone, battling against hundreds of them. It was enough for a book to awaken my interest, for that very same book to become the object of the rats' hunger. And precisely the books that I enjoyed most, those which I most ardently wished to preserve, became my enemies' favourite prey. There was no hiding place they did not uncover or barrier they could not cross. That was when I realized that, if the rats were wiser than I was, I had no other choice but to learn their ancient wisdom. If my books were condemned to be the fodder of these beasts, then I was going to be the most ravenous beast of the pack. I read for days on end. Every time I finished a page, I would tear it out, stuff it in my mouth, and devour it in one bite. I soon learned to distinguish the taste and nutrient qualities of each author, each text, each school and each movement. And in my constant battle against the rats, the more I resembled them, the more human I felt. Just as Homo sapiens *evolved from consumption of raw flesh to cooked meat, so I passed from devouring books to savouring them. And since below the library there was a wine cellar as well stocked as the bookshelves, I discovered that for every author there was one corresponding wine, one perfectly complementary accompaniment.*

During one of my first meals, I feasted on an early edition of Don Quixote *in Spanish; that very night, delighted with Señor Cervantes, I dined on his* Exemplary Novels. *And the next day, so fascinated was I with my find, I breakfasted on a French translation of the book that I had to tear out of the rats' teeth. I followed that with a first edition of* Werther *and with* The Arabian Nights. *After Montaigne's* Essays, *I tasted Philippe de Comines, the Marquise de Sévigné and the Duc de Saint-Simon. I am still saving the three last pages of the* Decameron *and of* Gargantua: *I enjoyed them so much that I am loath to finish them. I gulped down the poems of Everadi together with Ariosto, Ovid, Virgil, Catullus, Lucretius and Horace. I also tasted the delicious but hard to digest* Discours de la méthode, *followed by the* Traité des passions de l'âme. *As you will have realized, I do not enjoy rereading a book. However, I do possess what I would define as an organic memory: beyond the unpleasant gift of total recall (I could recite the* Odyssey *from beginning to end) something which is commonly called 'knowledge' has taken root, not in my spirit but in my body, not as a wealth of information*

but as a sum of instincts, in the animal sense of the word.
Literature, Dr Polidori, is my natural method of sur-
vival. I recommend that you try it: try eating the books
you read.

John Polidori was astonished. Many times he had re-
gretted his deficient memory. How often had he wished to
be able to recite a line of poetry on the appropriate occasion.
But his memory was conceptual, not literal. He could
remember with precision an idea, but he found it impossible
to adapt that idea to the metre and rhyme with which the
poet had conceived it. The few times he had tried to engage
a potential audience, he had lost his way in histrionic
gestures and in verses that refused to rhyme or scan. Now
Polidori had brought with him to the Villa Diodati
Wordsworth's *The Excursion*, and he thought that this might
make a good subject with which to begin the experiment.
He read the first page avidly, ripped it out, crumpled it and
put it in his mouth. It wasn't easy to chew on the dry paper:
it felt tough and the sharp edges cut his gums. At first, he
just wasn't able to swallow it down. He felt like a cow
chewing the cud; the miserable paper would not soften.
Finally, after several attempts that brought him to the edge
of nausea, he managed to push it down. As the page
descended his gullet, he felt like a boa that had swallowed a
whole lamb. He tried a second page. After the fifth, he
found the paper slipping down as easily as a bowl of broth.

Having reached page 93, Polidori was nearing the end of his gluttonous repast when he saw the door open and Byron walk in unannounced. For a long moment both men remained motionless, staring at each other. Polidori had his mouth full of paper and the corner of a page poked through his inky lips; on his lap was what was left of the book: the limp cover and a few remaining pages. He finished chewing and swallowed noisily, trying to hide what could not be hidden. Before turning on his heel and leaving the room, Byron whispered:

'*Bon appétit!*'

Polidori's only answer was a helpless little burp, dry, bitter and much too quiet to constitute a literary opinion.

III

DURING THE COURSE OF MY UNDER-
ground excursions, I found by chance some-
thing so utterly amazing that it became for
me a true revelation. In the corridors
adjacent to the narrow tunnel that joins Notre Dame
with Saint Germain des Prés underneath the Seine, I
frequently sensed the irresistible proximity of paper and
ink which, because of the intensity of the scent, I
guessed was lying expectantly in orgiastic quantities. It
was not, however, the smell of printer's ink but rather
the unmistakable perfume of manuscripts that attracted
my attention. With little difficulty, I found the passage-
way that finally led me to the source of this tempting
aroma. As far as I could make out, this was the cellar of
the Galland Bookshop and Publishing Company.
Suddenly, before my eyes, appeared the most dazzling

treasure I have ever seen: hundreds of thousands of handwritten volumes rising from the floor to the ceiling. It took me a while to realize their worth. They were not, as you might suppose, the originals of books that had achieved glory and fame in print, but on the contrary, those which bore the most terrible punishment to which a literary work may be condemned: each manuscript carried a red stamp on its front page that read in lapidary letters: 'UNPUBLISHABLE'. If I could only describe the marvels revealed to me in those pages condemned to death even before being born . . . I assure you that the history of Western literature would be transformed and made more glorious if even a few of these pages were to see the light of day in print — instead of many other well-known tomes that are now acknowledged as classics.

I was intrigued to find out the identity of the anonymous judge of all this unpublished literature, who decided, in our name, in the name of all readers, what would live and what would die. Thus I discovered one of the most secretive and eccentric characters ever to inhabit the bowels of this earth.

The man responsible for the fate of these unpublished manuscripts had occupied a sordid office in the bookstore's basement. Behind what had been his seat rose a machine of gigantic dimensions that took up almost the entire space of the room. This anonymous judge had completed what was perhaps the most thorough classifi-cation ever of the great novels of the world. He had analysed, numbered and counted each syntactic and grammatical element in the world's greatest books, word by word, from the earliest Oriental tales such as Lady Murasaki's Genji Monogatori *and the anonymous* Kalila and Dimna, *to Petronius'* Satyricon *and the* Canterbury Tales, *to* Don Quixote *and the* Exemplary Novels, *not forgetting, of course, Boccaccio, Quevedo, Lope de Vega, Defoe, Swift, Lasage, Lafayette and Diderot. Scrutinizing these works he had classified each of their components (the number of pages and words, their weight, definite and indefinite articles, nouns, verbs, adjectives, prepositions, etc., etc., etc.) and had calculated their respective percentages. He had also taken into consideration the non-quantifiable components which he called generically the 'spiritual content'. He had decided that it was possible to objectify these components by subjecting the volumes to various treatments. For example: he crushed the books in enormous presses, he exposed them to very high temperatures, he immersed them in steam, he shook them violently, and by these methods he discovered that the books that did not change their weight during the experiments were the ones that had the best survival rate throughout the ages. Assuming that this peculiarity was a general law, he had devised what he called 'the Reading Machine'.*

At the base of the machine was a large cauldron heated with burning coals and attended by a stoker. Two colossal chimneys pierced the ceiling of the office and rose high above the publishing company's roof. At the back of the machine was a small door through which the manuscript was inserted. The first step was to weigh the book. If its weight fell within the acceptable parameters, it was moved to a page-counter equipped with a roller that had as many teeth as the stipulated number of pages. If the manuscript passed the 'formal tests', it went on to the so-called 'spiritual chamber' where it underwent various other treatments to 'objectify' its contents. If the book passed all these tests, it was automatically stamped in blue ink with the word 'PUBLISHABLE' and it concluded its progress down a long tube that led to the printers. If, on the other hand, the manuscript did not fulfil one of the machine's established standards, it was dropped into the black mouth of a vent that led down to the deepest cellars, carrying a red stamp with the word 'UNPUBLISHABLE'.

The anonymous editorial judge had evidently invented the machine with the sole purpose of saving time and avoiding the effort of reading so many books. Nevertheless, he was not driven by sloth; on the contrary, his intention was to gain more hours to carry on with his secret aspiration, the task that was to justify his shadowy existence: all he wanted was to write the perfect novel. He was of course the sole possessor of the magic formula. It took him ten years to write his book, which he called The Key to the Secret. *The glorious day came at last when he wrote the final word. All he really needed to do was to carry it to the printer himself, since he was the only deciding judge. But the temptation was too strong. He opened the door of his machine and with a satisfied smile allowed his book to take the path of integrity. But then, to his horror, he saw the machine that he had invented spit out his precious manuscript with scornful haste, condemning it to the hell of the books in the cellar.*

Aghast, the stoker had no time to prevent the judge from entering his own machine in pursuit of his life's work.

I have seen with my own eyes the unfortunate judge's corpse lying on top of his manuscript in the deepest of the cellars. And on his forehead, I could make out the same lapidary words that were stamped in scarlet letters on the front page of his magnum opus: 'UNPUBLISHABLE'.

I V

DURING MY FIRST YEARS I LED A LIFE OF peaceful retreat. I was completely happy. I had my very own paradise. Everything I wanted was within my reach. My nightly underground excursions allowed me to visit all the libraries of Paris and to devour the most exotic books in as many foreign languages as I had taught myself to decipher. I needed no one. However, as I approached the age of womanhood, a terrible thing happened.

From morning to night, as suddenly as a caterpillar turns into a moth, something in me changed. Something that would constrain me to abandon the utter solitude in which I felt so at ease and that would drive me to depend instead on my 'fellow' human beings. The day on which I became a woman, I was possessed by an overwhelming urge to know (in the purest biblical sense) a man. This was not like those flushes of arousal that so frequently came over me, not at all like the dampness low down that certain books would bring about. I knew full well how to console myself: I could manage splendidly alone and, to tell the truth, I much preferred my own meticulous caresses (no one knew my anatomy as well as myself) to the idea that a man might one day touch me. But this new feeling was utterly unfamiliar and purely physiological: if I had to compare it to some other physical need, I would be tempted to say it was as basic as hunger or thirst. I felt that, if I did not have a man, I would perish as surely as if I were deprived of food or drink. And after a few days of suffering this terrible urge, I found out that this was not an idle metaphor. My health deteriorated to the point where I was barely able to move. As you will guess, the decline of my sisters' health followed mine and, as my agony advanced, so did theirs.

My sisters were two beautiful young ladies. And their beauty matched their precocious ravenous lust. I myself had seen, through the bars of the air vent, how they lent themselves willingly to the lascivious games of Monsieur Pelian, my father's business partner, to whom had been entrusted my sisters' musical education. Monsieur Pelian would take advantage of my father's absences to pay my sisters a visit. As I said, his were lascivious and obscene games, but nothing more than games. Monsieur Pelian would sit my sisters on his lap, one on each knee. First he would tell them a story, somewhat vulgar and sufficiently risqué to make them blush, supposedly with shame, but in fact with sheer excitement. Monsieur Pelian was obviously utterly transported by his two identical dolls, as if what moved him were not their beauty but their perfect similarity. Monsieur Pelian's favourite game was called 'Spot the Differences'. The twins had told him that there were only four tiny differences between their two bodies and, since Monsieur Pelian had never discovered for certain which one was Colette and which Babette, he felt obliged to tell them apart through his sense of touch. He would begin by caressing one of my sisters' blond curls. With delicate pianist's fingers he would touch first the back of a neck, then draw a line down to the top of the spine, after which, like an expert wine taster, he would brush his lips against the tip of an ear, which would make the sister thus honoured shut her blue, transparent eyes and let out an almost imperceptible sigh. He would then trail his tongue along the Egyptian perfection of her neck down to the curve of a shoulder. After that, he would withdraw, leaving my sister trembling like a leaf, thirsty for more, and repeat his ministrations on the other one, with identical results.

'Up to this point, I've found no differences whatsoever,' he would say in a hoarse whisper, and

he would carry on with his examination.

Monsieur Pelian would sit on the piano bench and pull one of my sisters towards him; kindly, he would ask her to stand in front of him and, without touching her, he would beg her to turn round very slowly. Then Monsieur would inspect her with hungry eyes, looking first at her torso in profile, where the nipples of her budding breasts would stiffen under his gaze and become visible through the dress. Then, as my sister turned, he would glue his eyes to her firm but childish buttocks; my sister would then lean forward to emphasize their curve and she would back up closer to Monsieur's flaring nostrils. However, he would not touch her buttocks but instead he would move his hands up her thighs until his fingers almost reached her hot and humid sex. At that point, he would gently push her away and ask my other sister to come before him. With similar results he would repeat the scene.

'Neither do I find differences here,' he would mutter with feigned annoyance. 'I shall have to continue investigating.'

The longed-for moment now arrived. He would beg my sisters to sit side by side on top of the piano. He would slowly lift their skirts, caressing first their firm ankles and then, taking in his hands one foot of each, he would rub the twin soles against his member which, by then, was willing and ready, and pressed obscenely against his trousers. In this position, Monsieur Pelian would pass his tongue along my sisters' skin from one foot to the other, and then to the silent and moist lips that seemed to beg with slight tremors for his familiar caresses. While he licked the small red mound that peered between the folds of one of my sisters' sex, he would insert and withdraw first a single finger, then two and three, in the sweet fiery crevice of the other. In the meantime, my sisters would kiss one another and caress each other's nipples. Just before they reached their climax, Monsieur would stand up, take a few steps back and watch them, breathless and bathed in sweat.

'I still can't find any difference,' he would say in an upset tone. Then he would rearrange his clothes, turn on his heels and leave. From the door he would say his farewells:

'Perhaps we'll be luckier next time. Practise what I taught you today.'

He would close the door softly and my sisters would remain staring at each other on top of the piano, their legs open, their sex moist and their breasts aroused.

V

MONSIEUR PELIAN SEEMED TO BE THE ONLY
one who could give us what we needed. But
would it be wise to reveal to him my existence?
What would become of the Legrand sisters –
and of their father – if it were suddenly revealed that
they were hiding a monstrous sibling? How could we tell
that the authorities would not decide that I should be
locked away in seclusion? What if I were to become the
object of abominable experiments at the hands of
morbid physicians? Nevertheless, the most pressing
question was, how would we convince Monsieur Pelian
to give himself to my monstrous person? However
perverse he might have been, however convoluted his
prurient imagination, it was not likely that his lust
would make him desire a foetus covered in the fur of a
sewer rodent, an inhuman freak, a compound of the

most loathsome beasts from the murkiest depths. Most probably, if confronted by me, Monsieur would take to his heels and scream out to all and sundry that he had seen a hideous monstrosity: or, more likely, he would simply die of fright. We decided, my sisters and I, that the only possible solution was to play another game that Monsieur enjoyed: Blind Man's Buff.

My sisters took to their beds. In despair, my father decided to call the doctor. But they fervently asked him not to and, instead, begged for his associate to come. Without understanding why, our father gave in to their extravagant pleas. As for me, I spent two whole days agonizing behind the vent that led to my sisters' room.

My father returned with Monsieur Pelian who, distressed and concerned, remarked on my sisters' weakness and pallor. Babette begged our father to leave them alone with Monsieur Pelian for a moment. My father, who had never had reason to suspect the honourable intentions of his associate since he had entrusted him with his daughters' education, must have imagined that my sisters required a confessor, in order to expiate their childish faults and state their final wishes. He embraced his associate and friend and, fighting back his tears, left the room.

Monsieur Pelian, standing between the two beds, stared at the girls in anguished bewilderment.

'My children,' he began, 'as soon as your father told

me of your illness I came without delay. I don't know how I can be of service to you,' he said, much moved, kneeling down. 'I am not a doctor. But you may ask of me whatever you wish.'

With difficulty, Babette propped herself up on her elbows and motioned for him to bring his ear to her lips.

'We want to play Blind Man's Buff.'

Monsieur thought that Babette was delirious, and said, as he caressed her golden curls:

'My child, you don't know what you are saying . . .'

'We know perfectly well what we are saying,' Colette interrupted in a hoarse but imperious voice. 'We beg you, consider it our last request.'

'Please, do not refuse us this,' Babette said sweetly, putting on the innocent and yet perversely lascivious face that always so stirred Monsieur Pelian's darkest instincts.

'But if your father were to enter,' the piano teacher murmured, 'imagine, you sick like this, and I . . .'

'Bolt the door and come here,' Babette whispered, placing her index finger on Monsieur Pelian's lips, certain in the knowledge that he had already given in.

Colette put a blindfold around Monsieur Pelian's eyes.

'No cheating, now. No spying.'

The game consisted of having Monsieur guess which

of the two sisters was touching him. If he made a mistake, his penalty was to take off an article of clothing. My sisters sat on the edge of one of the beds and placed Monsieur in between them.

First Babette brushed her tongue over the rim of Monsieur Pelian's lips.

'Oh you naughty girl, I recognize your breath. You are Colette.'

My sisters lacked the strength to laugh.

'First mistake. You must take off your waistcoat.'

Slowly they undid the waistcoat buttons, one by one from top to bottom, and when they reached the last one, they could not prevent themselves from deliberately brushing the shape that had begun to appear under Monsieur's trousers. Then Babette put her finger inside his mouth.

'I have no doubt now, that finger is Babette's,' said Monsieur Pelian with absolute certainty.

There was no time for honesty or for teasing out the game as they used to do; instead, they took the most expedient route.

'Once again, the answer is no. Now the shoes.'

Breathing heavily, one of my sisters took off his left shoe and the other the right one. According to the rules, each of the shoes should have been a separate penalty. But given the circumstances, Monsieur did not object. He was truly concerned that his friend might come upon them; paradoxically, this threat seemed to excite him even more. Colette now put both hands on his groin, surrounding Monsieur Pelian's prominent fly.

Impressed by the size and the movements of the trapped animal, my sisters began prodding and grabbing and finally, totally forgetting the rules of the game, they threw themselves on the piano teacher. Babette sat on his face and ordered him to put his tongue up her burning crevice. Colette undid his fly and freed Monsieur's large member whose diameter, she noticed, could barely fit in her small mouth.

It was then that I descended from the vent and with my scant remaining strength added myself to the two. Babette made sure that the blindfold was secure and that it hid Monsieur Pelian's eyes completely. At the right moment, Colette offered me what she held in her hands and I drank down to the last drop the delicious elixir, abundant and warm. And while I drank, I could feel my body, as if by magic, once more filling up with life.

By the time Monsieur Pelian had taken off his blindfold, I was back in my beloved library. Astonished, the piano teacher saw that the two poor angels, who a few moments before had barely had the strength to speak, now looked bursting with life, their cheeks pink with health.

When our father re-entered the room and saw that his daughters were well again, he embraced his friend, kissed his hands, and seemed on the point of falling to his knees.

'This time I'm certain, there's no question: you are William,' said Monsieur Pelian, exhausted and confused, so as to bring the game to a close.

VI

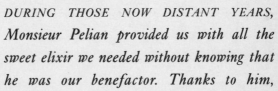*DURING THOSE NOW DISTANT YEARS, Monsieur Pelian provided us with all the sweet elixir we needed without knowing that he was our benefactor. Thanks to him, Babette and Colette grew in both stature and beauty and very soon turned into two stunning young women.*

When Monsieur Pelian aged and declined, my sisters discovered how to take advantage of the now unattractive old man. The piano teacher had many solid friendships in the select circles of the theatre. Indeed, my sisters were more gifted for drama than for music, and under his patronage it was easy for them to join the Théâtre-sur-le-Théâtre, a company housed on the Rue Casimir-Delavigne.

My father did not approve of his daughters consorting in these circles which he suspected were not entirely wholesome. However, thanks to the insistence of his old friend, he ended up giving his consent though against his will, at least in the beginning. The company's director was a certain Monsieur Laplume, a man whose professional judgement was often tainted by his irrepressible affection for women. Indeed, it was not long before the director fell prey to the identical charms of Babette and Colette. Since he was much younger than Monsieur Pelian, my sisters quickly agreed that they had found the perfect substitute for their now decrepit piano teacher.

My sisters discovered in this new friend a fiery and attractive lover very much to their liking, and yet they saw their relationship as strictly utilitarian: not only did he assure them of a regular dose of vital fluid, but he eased their ascent up the often arduously competitive steps of the thespian hierarchy, until they reached the first rank among the prima donnas. The time it took them to climb from the lowest to the highest echelon was brief; their talents, alas, were modest. My sisters quickly earned the indignant dislike of all the women in the company and, in inverse proportion, the fascinated admiration of all the men. In spite of their youth, whatever their methods, the Legrand sisters had now become famous actresses. They had no trouble seducing whatever man they chose; on the contrary, their gentleman callers were numerous and waited in long lines at the door of their dressing room, or huddled under the awning at the exit of the theatre. And, as you can well imagine, the inevitable happened.

As was to be expected, together with their fame came a deluge of wedding proposals. Monsieur Laplume was driven to literally kicking the beaus out into the street from where they stood drooling in the wings, their arms laden with flowers and gifts. And yet, in spite of his efforts, the angry director was unable to prevent a pair of gallants from winning my sisters' hearts, the two almost at the same time. The Legrand sisters had fallen in love with a couple of young brothers.

I had suddenly become nothing but a hated obstacle. Not only because my sisters did not show the slightest intention of sharing with me the fruit of their beloved, but also because my existence made the much-desired state of matrimony an unattainable illusion. Of necessity, though much against our will, we three were forced to remain together. How then could they conceive of forming separate homes? My sisters seriously debated the possibility of confessing to their fiancés my monstrous existence. But how could they be certain that these men would not flee in horror when faced with the hideous revelation that their two beautiful brides were part of an abominable trinity? And even if this last obstacle were overcome, how could they burden the brothers with the knowledge that there was no telling *what shape the fruit of their loins might acquire? What if they were to foster on earth a new race of monsters such as ourselves? My sisters' hatred towards me became so intense that, were it not for the fact that their own lives depended on my own, they would have killed me without further thought. I cannot say I blamed them.*

Dr Polidori, I lack the words to tell you of my torment and my guilt. And without wishing to take on the airs of a martyr, had I not known that my death would have such terrible consequences, I would have put an end to my days myself. But I do not wish to seem melodramatic.

My sisters made a cruel decision. They renounced love for ever. However, for the same reason that I could not kill myself, they could not renounce sex. They broke up with their beaus without offering an explanation, thereby condemning their loved ones to lifelong suffering. I feel obliged, therefore, to speak out in favour of my sisters, in the face of the gossip that dishonours their reputation, and say that their lives are unjustly branded as 'loose' and are in reality the result of the purest and most difficult act of renunciation: a farewell to love. This paradoxical gesture of self-denial explains their hasty, detached and indifferent attitude towards their affairs of the heart. If my sisters sought relationships with lowly men who lacked all spiritual adornment, they did so with the sole intention of never becoming enamoured again.

Dr Polidori, if I take it upon myself to reveal to you these intimacies of my sisters' lives, I do so only with the intention of cleansing their sullied reputation. Having said this and having restored both their good name and their honour, I shall not indulge in any further such confidences. I shall describe only those that concern our own affairs: yours and mine, Dr Polidori.

VII

THE YEARS DID NOT PASS IN VAIN. I SHALL spare you the longer version of our biographies. My sisters' lasting beauty was finally defeated by the merciless advance of time. Their magnificent and proud bosoms lost volume and consistency, and became deflated sacks. Their buttocks, traditional emblems that once might well have been part of the Legrand coat of arms, spread and sagged. No creams or lotions could hide the deep wrinkles that multiplied day by day. Immersion in warm milk no longer effaced the brown spots that progressively covered their skin, once their pride and joy but now increasingly resembling the hide of an elephant. Slowly, the dozens of handsome gentlemen who once paid court began to desert them. Their oldest and most faithful lovers lost their masculine ardour and, in many cases, simply died of old age. In a word, my sisters were now decrepit hags no longer able to make use of a man since, even with ready cash, they were incapable of arousing the virility of their lovers. Yet they had to keep up appearances because, as you well know, it is one thing to be the subject of unconfirmed rumours that can be indignantly refuted, and quite another to be exposed in a public scandal. Dr Polidori, we had reached a crisis point, because for weeks we had not been able to bring to the house a single drop of the vital liquid. My sisters (I tell this full of vicarious shame) went to the extreme of dressing up as beggars and visiting nearby brothels, searching among their rubbish for sheaths that might contain even a drop of the source of life. Of course, this was not sufficient: it was like trying to quench the thirst of a bedouin lost in the desert with a tear born out of his own despair.

We were dying.

PART III

I

The First Victim

PARIS HAD BECOME A HOSTILE AND dangerous city. France remembered well the Legrand sisters and, even old and decrepit, they were recognized by passers-by. And even if their libertine reputation had lent them a certain glamour and mystery, they could not very well exhibit themselves as a pair of aged nymphomaniacs, desperately trying to find a man in the lower districts of Paris. Realizing that under the circumstances their best plan was to seek anonymity, my sisters decided to abandon Paris. I cannot tell you what terrible humiliations I was forced to undergo every time we set off on a journey! To avoid showing the world my monstrous features, my sisters had bought a travelling cage for dogs. How many hours have I suffered, locked up in that cell that barely held my poor (allow me the liberty) human body. What distances have I not crossed in the luggage rack of a coach and, even worse, in the filthy bowels of a ship, travelling among beasts!

We visited almost all the great cities of Europe. My sisters hoped to find a pair of lovers who would provide them with what we needed and they looked forward to a life of quiet anonymity and peaceful happiness: indeed, the life all unmarried women wish for. In elegant Budapest, our first destination, they dressed in their French finery and walked along the Danube, on the imposing bank of Buda; that night they ended up collecting sheaths outside the brothels on the sordid bank of Pest, and bearing in silence their humiliation. In London they had even worse luck, and in Rome they fell victim to the cruellest indignities. Madrid was a calamity and in St Petersburg they almost perished from the cold. They then told themselves, with practical reasonableness, that their best chance lay not in the big cities but in the peace and quiet of the country. If solitary shepherds, condemned to forced abstinence, were allowed by their baser instincts to enjoy the company of their cursed sheep, how could my sisters possibly be worse received than in the cities? They admitted that they were old, but however much past their prime they might be, it was unthinkable that they should not be preferred to foul-smelling woolly beasts. But since precaution is a wise counsellor, to better their chances, they did teach themselves how to bleat.

THUS WE DECIDED TO SETTLE IN A MODEST *but charming chalet in the Swiss Alps.*

I am inclined to believe that our first victim was the result of a tragic conjunction between lust and the need for survival.

Our caretaker was a young and handsome man, a strong peasant, son of Welsh immigrants whose rustic manners lent him a certain savage charm. Derek Talbot (for such was his name) lived in a small hut not far from our home. From our window, my sisters, hidden behind the flowerpots, took to watching him incessantly. Perhaps because of his bucolic innocence and his deeply rooted bond with the earth, he used thoughtlessly to take off his shirt to mow the lawn, a spectacle that troubled us (for want of a better word) because his torso seemed sculpted by Phidias and his strong arms appeared to be as solid as the limbs of a wild animal. Every time he wielded his clippers, his muscles would bulge in an obscene way and we could not help but picture to ourselves his member, which we imagined to be as willing to please as his arms were willing to work. But our understandable excitement was nothing compared to our desperate need to obtain, in whatever way possible, the vital fluid. However much I tried to distract my thoughts with a book, I could not subdue my longing to see the white elixir spurt like a torrent of lava, and this image would recur with the wilful insistence of bad thoughts. I could imagine myself drinking its warmth to my fill. Enforced abstinence, I must tell you, had weakened me, as it had my sisters, to the point when it would soon cause physical agony unless the elixir were obtained.

With time running out, in spite of their ebbing strength my sisters were forced to proceed with great care. Their plan was, if nothing else, ingenious. They had kept, from their days of stardom, an ancient handbill that they used to gaze at, full of nostalgia. It showed them, young and dazzling, completely naked and kissing each other, their hands on their nipples. Now their idea was to leave this handbill casually lying around in an envelope, as if by accident, so as to attract the eye of Derek Talbot. There were two possible outcomes. The first and most ambitious was that the lascivious picture would awake in him a desire for the scene's protagonists, even though it depicted their long-gone days of glory. Perhaps, recognizing in the two aged women some trace of their past beauty, he might submit himself willingly to the present-day Babette and Colette. The second possibility was that, because of the abstinence to which his remote dwelling condemned him, Derek Talbot might be tempted by the picture to indulge in solitary satisfaction, at which point, with amazingly good timing, we would pounce on the precious fruit of his forbidden pleasure.

III

*THAT SAME AFTERNOON, WHILE THE CARE-
taker was finishing his gardening, Babette
entered his hut and left the picture on his night
table. The hut had a sloping roof and from our
house we could look down and see Derek Talbot's bed
through the skylight. When night had fallen, Babette
stealthily climbed up a ladder to the caretaker's roof.
Colette, as planned, leaned out of a window of our
house, from where she could see the distant silhouette of
Babette, like a cat in heat, cut out against the sky.*

*The young man had taken off his clothes and, sitting
on the edge of his bed, had just lit a candle when he
suddenly noticed the envelope. Through the skylight,
Babette observed how he examined with surprise first
the back and then the front, and then how he tried to
decipher what he could see of the picture that showed*

through it. He knew that the envelope was not addressed to him, but he could not restrain his curiosity. He drew out the picture a little further and seemed to recognize the face he had uncovered. In fact it took him several minutes to understand that the vaguely familiar features belonged to one of the elderly lodgers, but this suspicion was confirmed when, after drawing out the picture a little further still, he revealed the identical features of the other old lady. Babette saw how Derek Talbot's eyes popped out of his head in amazement at the full handbill; then she observed with a mixture of anxiety and excitement how the caretaker fell back on the bed, his eyes glued to the picture and his member beginning to rise. His hand slid shyly downwards and, as if driven by an independent will, or at least by one that was not his own, reached its goal. Babette smiled lasciviously and licked her lips like a hungry animal. With one hand Derek Talbot placed the picture on his pillow and with the other he began to caress himself. My sister, on tiptoes on the roof, lifted her skirts and wet her fingers; then she slowly touched her hardened prominent nipples and with her other hand circled her sex, to the rhythm of the young man's caresses, holding back or increasing the rhythm according to Derek Talbot's tempo, not willing to attain her climax either before or after the young caretaker. At the very moment he was about to reach an orgasm that promised to be prodigious

*both in quality and in the quantity of the craved fluid
produced, two things happened simultaneously. The
young man's eyes settled by chance on the crucifix that
hung over his bed and, as if he had been surprised in his
foul deed, he felt the finger of God threatening him
with the fiercest torments of hell. Terrified, the caretaker stopped what he was doing, flung the picture away
from him, covered his sex (which had in the meantime
dwindled to nothing) and began to cross himself and
beg the Lord's forgiveness. My sister, bewildered,
remained frozen where she was, half-kneeling, one
finger still inside and another somewhere between her
lips and her breasts. It was as if she were pointing to herself and saying to the world, 'Behold, I am the greatest
of fools.' She looked like an allegory of Decadence,
perched up there on the roof in the middle of the night,
a pathetic effigy with her buttocks bare to the wind. As
if this were not bad enough, Derek Talbot, furious with
himself, slammed his fist on the night table so hard that
the heavy candlestick flew upwards with the force of a
bullet, hitting the frame of the skylight. The glass pane
swung on its hinges, and with bad luck it hit Babette
right on the chin, causing her to tumble into the hut,
sailing down buttocks foremost, crumpled and dishev-
elled. The young man, looking up, was petrified with
terror, and thought that this must be God's curse
descending from the heavens like an obscene (Babette's*

finger was still in place) and devastating comet. He had barely managed to raise his arms to protect himself when Babette's body hit him with full force.

My sister Colette, who was waiting at the window for a sign, was unable to make sense of the scene unfolding before her eyes. However, judging by the clamour, she suspected all had not gone well. She rushed downstairs, grabbed the rifle that hung above the hearth and, like a gunfighter, ran towards the caretaker's hut. This was to herald the onset of the tragedy.

IV

COLETTE, RIFLE IN HER HAND, ENTERED THE hut like an avenging angel. Brandishing the gun in front of her, she saw at the barrel's end the naked and terrified caretaker lying on his bed next to Babette who, dazed and confused, was trying to pick herself up.

Then, while Colette kept the rifle pointed at the poor young man, Babette tied him by the wrists and ankles to the four posts of the bedstead. As a precaution, they took down the crucifix and made ready to extract from the caretaker the nectar of life.

Derek Talbot saw my sister Colette put the rifle to his head with a face wild with excitement and desperation, and heard her barking at him to cooperate. My sisters had suddenly become nothing but a vulgar pair of robbers. However, my dear Dr Polidori, as you can well imagine, their strange booty was not easy to obtain. The *work of a thief is, as I conceive it, easy: if under the same circumstances a pair of improvising burglars had wanted to steal money or precious objects, their task would have been very simple. Even if the victim needed to be forced to reveal the location of the desired loot, it would be enough to threaten him firmly and with conviction. I suspect that a rifle pointed at his head would be sufficient persuasion. But now my sisters discovered that their quarry was more elusive than that. Objects, like confessions, pleas and tears, can be elicited from someone who is in your power. But how to lay your hands on that which lies beyond the victim's own will? Women (I do not include myself) may simulate pleasure and even fake an orgasm. But you men are barred from false pretences. How to stimulate an erection when, for whatever reason, your unhelpful partner refuses to be drawn into the adventure? And, of course, as we know, the male orgasm can never ever be faked. This was the desperate situation in which Derek Talbot found himself. The more my sisters demanded that he relinquish his precious treasure, the less was he able to comply. Far from attaining even a modest erection, he displayed a shamed shyness that transformed the proud and steady warrior (who a few minutes ago had stood rampant as a lion) into a sort of timid mouse that barely showed its tiny snout from the hairy nest of the pubis. My sisters could understand that the more strenuous their demands*

*on the young caretaker, the feebler their chances of ful-
filling their purpose. The scene now displayed in front of
Derek Talbot's eyes was certainly not erotically stimu-
lating: two crazed old women, one bruised and dazed,
stumbling erratically around the room and knocking
herself against the walls, and the other furiously pointing a rifle at his head. Colette decided to change her
strategy. First she made certain that the cords that
bound the caretaker's wrists and ankles were firmly
tied; then she left her weapon leaning against the wall;
finally, she walked up to the mirror and, sitting down
in front of it, inspected herself calmly. Without quite
knowing what she was doing, she patted her hair into
place and gradually felt her long-gone sensual talent
coming back to her, just as when she used to preen herself
in front of the dressing-room mirror before stepping out
on stage, in the springtime of her life. She thought she
could see in her clear eyes, now encroached upon by lines
and wrinkles, something of her old sensuality. She stared
down at her breasts and told herself that, in spite of the
passing years, she did not look all that bad and that, if
nothing else, her corset, tucking in the excess and filling
out the insufficiencies, lent her a buxomness that, though
illusory, was far from negligible. She crossed one leg over
the other and lifted her skirts above her thighs. She
wasn't kind to herself: she saw the flaccid flesh hanging
down in folds, considered the lumpy fat now occupying the*

place of the taut muscle which used to lend her legs the beauty of polished wood — and yet, in spite of the implacable devastation of time, she recognized in her aged body the nymph of days gone by. She told herself that if her own ruthless judgement, which used to torment her with its implacable severity, had now relaxed to allow a measure of leniency, why should it be unthinkable for her still to awaken a tiny spark of that ancient fire? She turned in her chair towards the young caretaker who had been observing her curiously, and she thought she saw in his look a glimmer of lust. She was not mistaken.

V

DEREK TALBOT WAS EXAMINING HER WITH *grudging approval. Colette suddenly felt beautiful. In her heart of hearts, she knew that she had always been more attractive than Babette and that only an idiot or a blind man would have confused her with her sister. She looked at Babette, who was still trying to compose herself, with sincere compassion. The caretaker paid no attention at all to Babette and instead kept his eyes fixed on the naked legs that Colette was displaying. My sister spread open her knees and, staring straight at Derek Talbot, first caressed her thighs and then leaned over to reach the rifle propped up against the wall. As she gently touched the barrel, she fixed her eyes on the young man's member (which seemed to be coming back to life) and lowered the rifle down to her pubis, holding it between*

her legs and brushing with her tongue the metal barrel. In this position, she swayed backwards and forwards, softly and languidly, as if on a rocking-horse. Derek Talbot had recovered the expression he had adopted while inspecting the old handbill. Colette, seeing that the caretaker's 'partner' had returned from the kingdom of the dead, stood up, approached the bed, sank down to her knees as if performing a deep curtsy, and took it in her hands, licking it from top to bottom and from bottom to top. Babette, beginning to recover her senses, watched the scene in disbelief. Colette, without letting go of her prey, lifted her eyes and looked at our sister with a pinch of malice, as if to say: 'I, Colette Legrand, have succeeded where you, decrepit old hag, never will.'

Colette felt a convulsion that you could call seismic in the member she held in her hands. Quickly she wrapped her trophy in a handkerchief and then, as if from an angry volcano, the much-desired white lava began to flow. When the tremors had ceased, Colette pressed harder to extract the very last drop. With the vital fluid safely in the improvised sack, Colette tied up the ends and tucked it away in her clothes. Derek Talbot was trembling like a leaf. Suddenly he opened his eyes. As if passing from the sweetest of dreams to the most horrible nightmare, he saw a pair of withered hags laughing at him like hyenas. Derek Talbot felt a profound disgust rising and turning into a wave of nausea. At first he begged them to free him, then he cursed them with all his strength, swearing to denounce them to the four winds and to let the world know that the Legrand sisters were nothing but a pair of whores.

Quickly, my sisters returned to the chalet and brought me the stolen nectar. As the life fluid descended my throat, our souls gradually returned to our bodies, until we were completely restored. From our house we could still hear Derek Talbot's cries and threats.

It was then that my sisters realized that if indeed the young man were to publicize what had happened, the rumours about them would be truly and irrevocably confirmed.

Full of new vitality and driven by a unanimous purpose, my sisters returned to Derek Talbot's hut. When the caretaker saw them enter, he burst into renewed and more terrible curses. Babette lifted the rifle, aimed it at the young man's forehead and pulled the trigger.

This was to be the beginning of a series of demented crimes.

VI

I AM INCLINED TO BELIEVE THAT MY sisters never thought of themselves as murderers. They killed with the same natural ease with which the tiger sinks its teeth into the neck of a gazelle. They killed without hatred, without cruelty. They killed without pity and without intent of redemption. They killed without method and without care. They felt neither remorse nor pleasure. They killed simply to follow the law of nature: because we had to live. We became nomads. We would arrive in a city or a town, my sisters would choose their victim, they would obtain the booty, they would kill two or three times, and then we would leave for a new destination. I have told you what torment these journeys were for me. My sisters, however, seemed pleased with their new life. Travel excited them. During a single year, we travelled more than you have done in your entire life. Chance took us from the western to the eastern tip of Europe, from Lisbon to St Petersburg, from north to south, from the Scandinavian kingdoms to the island of Crete. We saw exotic lands on both sides of the Atlantic, from the furthest edge of the South Seas and the shores of the River Plate to the United States of America. I admit I am unable to count, even approximately, the number of corpses we left in our wake.

Dr Polidori, as far as I'm concerned, I must tell you that I cannot continue to carry the heavy weight of my remorse, or the burden of my fatigue. I am a haggard monster. If I have taken the decision to confess to you my existence it is because I know that, in the deepest recesses of our souls, we are alike. I know that we can be of service to each other. What I can offer you in exchange for you-know-what is something that your heart has always longed for. I shall deliver it tomorrow. Now I must sleep, since I have not much strength left.

You shall hear from me again.

Annette Legrand

The light, far away on the top of the hill, was blown out.

PART IV

I

JOHN WILLIAM POLIDORI REREAD THE LAST paragraphs of the letter. Once again, he felt overwhelmed by fear. And yet his feelings were ambivalent. In his mind's eye, he pictured the corpses found in the vicinity of the Château de Chillon. Against his will he saw the body of Derek Talbot, hands and feet tied to the bed, stark naked, a hole in his head and drenched in his own blood. What terrified him most now, he realized, was not the ominous letters; on the contrary, they appeared to offer his only salvation from the murderous lust of the Legrand sisters. In spite of the dreadful history outlined in the last letter, Polidori was confident that he might draw some advantage from it. He asked himself whether Annette Legrand really knew what it was that his heart most desired, and he clung to the superstitious hope that indeed she might. He did not feel the slightest shame at the idea of revealing his deepest anxieties; no, he was more than willing to confess to her his unspeakable miseries. All of a sudden, Polidori understood that the abominable sister had the power, not only to shield him from death, but also to change his pitiful existence entirely. John Polidori folded the letter and slid it back into the envelope. With the eagerness of a man in love, he longed that the day might end (the day that had not yet begun) in order for him to receive the next letter. The possibility of sleeping had not even crossed his mind. He could not imagine how Annette Legrand managed to produce the letters on his desk, knowing that she did not allow anyone to see her. But in the hope that she would want to continue the correspondence, John Polidori discreetly withdrew from his room.

As the secretary was going downstairs, he looked out from the landing and was met with a desolate tableau: the room was lit by a funereal candelabrum, flickering dimly in the middle of the table. At the head, flanked by two suits of armour, sat Lord Byron, and across from him Percy Shelley. To either side, facing each other, were Mary and Claire. The glimmer from the hearth distorted the light from the candelabrum, lending the room the atmosphere of a witch's den. Byron's eyes shone with a wicked glint unfamiliar to Polidori. It was not clear whether Claire, her head un- naturally stiff, her hands on the table, was showing the whites of her eyes or her closed eyelids, because of the flick- ering of the flames. From his position on the landing,

Polidori could not see Mary's face but he could hear her agitated breath. Percy Shelley had lost his usual expression of amused cynicism and, for once, seemed to be terrified. In front of Byron lay an open book. With a deep voice, he read a passage that his secretary had never heard before:

> *'The lady sprang up suddenly,*
> *The lovely lady, Christabel! . . .*
> *The night is chill; the forest bare;*
> *Is it the wind that moaneth bleak? . . .*
> *Hush, beating heart of Christabel!*
> *Jesu, Maria, shield her well!*
> *She folded her arms beneath her cloak,*
> *And stole to the other side of the oak.*
> *What sees she there?'*

Polidori noticed that Shelley had grown pale and that a tremor was forcing him to grip the sides of his chair. Byron continued:

> *'Beneath the lamp the lady bowed,*
> *And slowly rolled her eyes around;*
> *Then drawing in her breath aloud*
> *Like one that shuddered, she unbound*
> *The cincture from beneath her breast:*
> *Her silken robe, and inner vest,*
> *Dropt to her feet, and full in view,*

Behold! her bosom and half her side –
A sight to dream of, not to tell!
O shield her! shield sweet Christabel!'

At that point in Coleridge's poem, Shelley let out a piercing scream, jumped from his chair and fell at Byron's feet, twitching and muttering unintelligibly. With great effort, the three others lifted him and carried him to the couch. Shelley was delirious. Drenched in cold sweat, his eyes rolling, he described the horrible visions that Byron's reading had conjured up. He spoke of a woman whose breasts bore, instead of nipples, a pair of menacing eyes.

Polidori, the invisible witness, was enjoying the sad spectacle of the young sceptic, normally so proud of his atheism, who was now, in the grip of fear, nakedly revealing his superstitious soul. Polidori decided to make his presence known, savouring in anticipation his revenge. He, the 'poor lunatic' according to Shelley, would now be recognized as the doctor, the one whose responsibility it was to heal that poor suffering creature who pretended to be a poet.

'What is all the commotion about?' he interrupted from the stairs, in the tones of a scholar disturbed from his studies.

Byron begged him to do something to help his friend. Polidori hurried downstairs and with pompous concern (meant to reveal the greatness of spirit which allowed him to forgive and forget former affronts) he leaned over the young man. And indeed Polidori's intervention had an immediate effect. Shelley's vacant look fell upon Byron's secretary just as he was about to take his pulse, and he immediately recovered his senses.

'Don't allow that miserable worm to touch me with his filthy hands!' he shouted, jumping to his feet and pulling away in disgust.

Obviously Shelley's pride was even stronger than the powerful effect of absinthe.

'He doesn't know what he is saying . . .' Polidori whispered to his lordship.

'I know perfectly well what I'm saying!' shouted Shelley as he rearranged his clothes and made his way back to the table. 'Let us continue,' he added, as if nothing had happened.

Mary drew near, put her arms around him and said softly:

'Perhaps we'd better rest . . .'

'I said I was perfectly all right. We shall continue with the reading.'

Mary sat down again obediently at the table. Byron, fearing that his friend would suffer a new crisis or, even worse, that his secretary might have a breakdown, decided to bring the evening to a close. His position was a difficult one, like that of King Solomon. If he put an end to the reading, he would be offending Shelley, and if he continued as if nothing had happened, he could imagine his secretary leaping from the veranda for the second time. Suddenly Byron's face lit up. He proposed that the evening be brought to a close on condition that each of those present, inspired by Coleridge's text, would agree to compose a fantastical tale of his or her own. In four days' time, at midnight exactly, they would convene again to read out their individual efforts.

Without intending to, Byron had just forced his secretary into the most heartless of duels: not possessing the right weapons, Polidori had not the slightest chance of emerging victorious against his clever opponent.

II

JOHN POLIDORI SPENT FOUR HOURS STARING at a page that persisted in remaining blank. He would dip his pen in the inkpot, shift in his chair, stand up, walk from one end of the room to the other, return quickly to his seat as if he had just caught hold of the right phrase with which to begin his story, only to find, as he was about to write it down, that the ink had dried on the tip of his pen. After he had finished removing the dry crust, he would discover that the words had evaporated like the spirit in a pigment. The scene repeated itself as in a nightmare.

John Polidori knew that he had his tale: there it was, at an arm's reach. And yet, for reasons that one might call practical rather than creative, he was unable to cross the threshold from the *res cogitans* of his prodigious imagination to the miserable *res extensa* of the paper. He came to hate the very

149

stuff the page was made of. This was his only obstacle: why did a soul such as his, an inhabitant of the lofty world of ideas, have to sink to the mundane slough of paper? The true poet had no need to leave a written testimony of that incommunicable experience that was Poetry. With this conviction, and the intuition that someone else would very soon solve his 'technical' problem, John William Polidori fell asleep at his desk, holding his pen in his hand.

III

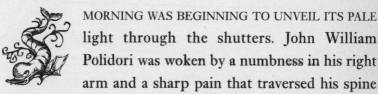MORNING WAS BEGINNING TO UNVEIL ITS PALE light through the shutters. John William Polidori was woken by a numbness in his right arm and a sharp pain that traversed his spine from end to end. He sat up in his chair, stretched his legs, propped them up on his desk, and would have gone back to sleep, were it not for a detail which he happened to notice. He did not remember having closed the shutters. He told himself that perhaps they had swung shut in the storm. But as he looked more closely he realized that no wind, however strong, could have bolted them shut as well. Automatically he let his eyes fall to the base of the candlestick. As he had suspected, he saw once again, in the appointed place, a black envelope stamped with a red seal and marked with the letter *L*. For the first time he felt like a hunted animal.

My dear doctor,

Good morning. I trust you feel restored. I did not wish to disturb you, so I have gone about my business very quietly. I saw you fast asleep and you looked like an angel. Seeing you thus, with a childlike expression on your face, I was filled with tenderness. I have taken the liberty of loosening your tie and pulling off your shoes. If the way you smiled at me in your sleep is any indication, I would say that you were grateful.

Polidori realized that he was indeed barefoot, but he recalled that he had not taken off his shoes the previous evening. Looking at himself in the mirror, he saw that his tie was hanging loose around the collar of his shirt. An attack of nausea forced him to bend over. Mechanically, he pulled off his tie and, holding it between two fingers, threw it in the wastepaper basket. Only then, as he leaned over, did he see in the very centre of his desk, next to the inkpot and the pen, a copious number of written sheets there where, the night before, he had abandoned his miserable blank page. For one second, he wondered whether he himself hadn't filled these sheets before falling asleep. Perhaps because of the number of pages, Polidori was slow in noticing that sitting on top of them was a tiny silver box fashioned in the rococo style, whose many whirligigs converged in the middle around a letter *L*, identical to that on the envelope's seal.

Afraid to touch even one of these gifts, as if wary of catching a lethal disease, Polidori decided to see whether the enigma could not be solved by reading the letter.

You know full well what is that 'something' you possess. But I have not yet told you what I can offer you in exchange. I know (as I have said) that which you desire the most. I would swear I even know that of which you have always dreamt, that which often keeps you awake and that which clouds your eyes in your reveries. I can guess that the bitter nourishment of your soul is the poison of envy. I know you would be willing to cut off a finger from your right hand for the sake of a couple of sonnets – and your whole hand for one complete story. I have no doubt that you would relinquish your soul to the devil for three hundred discreetly composed pages. Well then, what I request from you is not impossible. You will lose nothing at all when you give me that which I require in order to live. I am not asking for charity. Nor am I offering you eternal life. But what I am offering you is something very like it: future fame. Perhaps the only thing I have learned in my long existence is the art of writing. In exchange for that which I need, I shall grant you the authorship of a book that (have no doubt) will offer you free passage to the Olympus of Glory. You shall climb to the highest echelon of celebrity, higher even than that of the lord you serve. The pages you see on your desk are the first section of a tale. Consider this a gift. Read them: if you judge them worthless, throw them into the fire and I shall not bother you again — I can speak only for myself, not for my sisters. However, if you decide that you wish to put your name to this work, you shall give me what I need. If you say yes, this very night I shall deliver the second part. For each delivery I shall help myself once to what I require. The contents of the little box will simplify things.

Avidly, Polidori turned to the manuscript on his desk. The first paragraph amazed him. These lines were exactly the ones he had wanted to write not only on the previous evening, but his entire life. Word for word, phrase for phrase, the text was the one his hand had refused to put down on paper. This was certainly the story he had dreamt. And there it was, all his, for his glory and fame, for his future, the book that would lift him high above Lord Byron. At last he would be more than his lordship's despised and anonymous shadow! At last he would vindicate his father's name, which the old man had been unable to honour!

This was not plagiarism, he said to himself, nor was it theft. Was this text not to be the fruit of his own being? Would he not lend his seed to breathe life into the tale yet to be concluded? He would become (he said to himself) quite literally the newborn's father.

And furthermore, what other term except 'fiction' could one apply to this entire nightmare? Who would believe him if he ever told the truth?

John Polidori opened the small box. He inhaled a sweet perfume that promised pleasant dreams. Opium. He feared the hallucinations induced by absinthe and was terrified of the sensual excesses brought on by cannabis. But opium always induced in him only an angelic slumber. He knew that what he feared in cannabis was not the loss of control over his reason but, on the contrary, the sharpening of his critical judgement, the onset of what he himself described as 'cyclical thought', according to which a pleasant notion was immediately opposed by an unpleasant, punitive one. When under the influence of cannabis, Polidori would tell himself that the only way to avoid that threat to his conscience was through pain, physical suffering which would squash any self-criticism. He would then imagine himself choking to death or having an apoplectic fit. And however hard he would try to convince himself that it was all in his own mind, the ache in his chest or the palpitations of his heart would impose themselves as strongly as any real physiological symptom.

Opium, on the other hand, freed him completely from any self-criticism, and even more so when he slept fitfully, since Polidori's dreams were often interrupted by a sudden inexplicable anguish. He would then wake in a fright and not be able to fall asleep again or free himself from the feeling of unease. But opium produced a lucid dream-state that was paradoxically free from thought, a spiritual clarity that liberated him from the mediation of his body. Then, he became pure spirit. An idea. A dream dreamt by a perfect being.

I V

First Encounter

NIGHT HAD FALLEN WHEN JOHN POLIDORI SAT at his desk ready to begin the ceremony. He filled his pipe with a thimbleful of opium. Next he lay down, fully dressed, on his bed, and only then put a flame to the bowl. He inhaled, holding the first breath for several seconds, savouring the taste of the smoke. Outside his window, he saw the threatening mountains of solid blackness cut out against a louring sky. The clouds looked like floating cities about to fall on the world. A fierce wind was shaking the pine trees and lifting the dead leaves in quick gusts.

As Polidori struck a second match, a bolt of lightning lit up the lake and shortly afterwards the house trembled with the sound of thunder. It began to rain.

John Polidori caressed the pages that held the beginning of 'his' story and stretched out his legs. He let himself fall into a delicious stupor, feeling the smoke slowly slide down his throat as softly as his breath. He was inhaling the magical spirits who put his tortured body to sleep. He exhaled and, in the blue smoke, he rid himself, as in an intimate exorcism, of the horrible demons of everyday life. He clutched the pages to his breast.

John Polidori was crossing a strange threshold, in a lucid daydream that would transport him to heights never visited before. He saw himself climbing up a stone spiral. He realized that it was the magical *Rundetaarn*, the Round Tower of Scandinavian myth. It occurred to him that this construction, with no stairs, was the same as the one that King Christian IV had ascended on his winged horse. Now John Polidori too was riding a bronze-coloured steed that bore him to the tower's very top, from where he could see all the kingdoms on both sides of the Baltic. He inhaled once more, deeply and carefully. Now he saw himself crossing a hill of black trees on whose branches hung human skulls with owls' eyes in their sockets. He was not in the least afraid. On his galloping horse he entered a path signposted 'Villa Diodati'. He rode up a flight of steps and entered a large hall: from a great height he observed, with a mixture of pity and distaste, a number of tiny human beings fornicating in a tangled heap like a miserable pack of hyenas. Lord Byron, down on his knees, bathed in a fetid sweat, was licking Percy Shelley's tongue while entering Mary Shelley who, at the same time, was biting her sister Claire's nipples until they bled. But he, Polidori, the humiliated secretary, the son of a scrivener, the hypochondriac quack, the ridiculous Pollydolly, was now the hand of God Himself. Touched by divine wrath, he lifted his right fist towards heaven and, from thin air, drew a rod of iron and from the iron a sword. The horse reared up on its hind legs, then began to gallop across the red carpet, carrying Polidori in a circle around the terrified pack who were now weeping and begging for mercy. Skilful as a Cossack, he grabbed Lord Byron by the hair and with one precise blow of his sword decapitated him. Byron's head now hung, grimacing and still babbling, from John William Polidori's right hand. His lordship's eyes glanced up and down, left and right, until they met the sight of his own body that, oblivious of what had happened, had not stopped fornicating with Mary. The head began a mad soliloquy, pleading, cursing, crying, uttering piercing screams and laughing like a lunatic. Polidori, tired of its ranting, gagged his lordship's mouth with a handkerchief and stashed the head in one of his saddlebags.

From the top floor came strangely familiar whimpers. Polidori dismounted, flung the bag over his shoulder and climbed the stairs.

The moaning sounds came, as he could now make out, from his own room. He entered but saw no one.

'I was waiting for you,' said a warm female voice. Suddenly the chair by his desk swung round and John Polidori saw, enchanted, the most beautiful woman he had ever seen. She was completely naked, one leg flung over the arm of the chair. John Polidori was not especially attracted to women, and yet here was a creature even more beautiful to his eyes than Percy Shelley, whose charms (as Polidori had told himself with an objective resignation born of envy and lust) had no equal. In fact, she was the perfect female version of Percy Shelley.

'I am Annette Legrand,' she said and stretched out her hand which, until that moment, had rested on her lips.

John Polidori knelt at her feet and kissed her hand with devotion. From inside the saddlebag came the muffled groans of Byron's head, thrashing away like a dying fish.

Annette Legrand licked her index finger and with a sweet trail of saliva drew a path from her pink and swollen nipples down to the blond fleece of her pubis.

Without saying a word, she stood up, leaned over and kissed John Polidori on the lips. Then, pulling him up under the arms, she offered him the chair. The saddlebag was still moving about on the floor and Byron's voice, now pleading, became clearer, as if freed from the gag of the handkerchief. With his eyes still fixed on the object of his desire, Polidori grabbed the candlestick from his desk and threw it with deadly aim at the bag, which it hit to the sound of splintered bones. Unconcerned, Annette Legrand undid one by one the buttons of Polidori's fly and drew out the thin but pleasing trophy that looked for all the world like a shy mushroom. She stood up, took a few steps and then, without turning, handed Polidori a sheaf of handwritten pages. On the front was written *The Vampyre* and, further down, *Part II*.

'This is my share of the deal,' she said with a voice that reminded Polidori of the chords of a cello.

Byron's secretary closed his eyes, hugged the pages and pressed his cheek against them.

'Are you not going to read them?'

'It isn't necessary, it was enough to read the first part.'

Annette knelt at Polidori's feet to receive her share of the exchange.

V

JOHN POLIDORI, STILL CLUTCHING THE MANU-script, shivering and breathless, his legs wide open, glanced down at his small member which Annette Legrand was caressing with the tip of her tongue. The saddlebag containing Byron's head, which had been lying apparently lifeless next to the door, suddenly began to tremble once more, letting out a series of muffled groans.

John Polidori took pleasure in delaying the payment, a delay that made his sex quiver with brief convulsions. Annette Legrand could feel with her fingers the fluids rising and falling. At first she appeared desperate and anxious, then her anxiety turned into exasperation. The more she urged her lover to give her what he had promised, the less Polidori seemed willing to comply.

Finally, as if against his will, the secretary paid up. It was a volcanic and torrential contribution. A voluptuous remuneration which seemed, to Polidori, excessive. Annette Legrand drank from his fountain with the thirst of a woman lost in the desert, voracious as a beast, the whites of her eyes showing, as if in ecstasy.

Polidori clung to his pages, eyes clenched shut, trembling like a leaf.

His tremors hadn't stopped when he heard a rough, drunken voice that sounded as if it came from the bottom of a cave. Polidori opened his eyes, and suddenly saw before him the most loathsome sight he had ever come across. The woman who, moments ago, had surrendered her beauty at his feet, quickly stood up. To his utter horror, Polidori saw rise before him a sort of anthropomorphic reptile, a small creature covered in the fur of a rat. Annette Legrand scurried away towards the vent in the wall. She lifted the grille and, with a rodent's speed, lost herself in the secretive darkness of the villa's empty pipes. Polidori looked down at his own body with disgust and then vomited every last scrap in his stomach.

The mutterings of Byron's head became suddenly intelligible, as if it had been able to spit out the gag entirely. Polidori heard a cackle of malicious laughter. He turned and saw, standing in the doorway, his lordship's entire body, the head settled in its usual place.

'My poor Pollydolly . . .' Byron was saying, without being able to finish because of his uncontrollable laughter.

Byron opened the door further and, revealed behind his lordship's shoulders, Polidori saw Mary, Claire and Percy Shelley, choking with laughter at the sight of the pathetic creature bent double over a bundle of paper, naked and smeared with the contents of his own stomach.

V I

FOR THREE WHOLE DAYS JOHN POLIDORI remained locked in his room. Annette Legrand had kindly given him three small flasks which she was to collect punctually during the night while Polidori slept, after the shameful and tiresome business of filling them. In exchange, and with corresponding honesty, she would leave the agreed number of pages on his desk, next to the candlestick. When the agreement finally drew to an end, John Polidori had turned into a sorry sight indeed.

Certainly the flasks that, it had been stipulated, were to be filled to the brim were of such a generous size that they managed totally to deplete Byron's young secretary. John Polidori was pale with deep purple rings under his eyes and a tremor in his right hand by the time he at last reached the end of the story.

He read and reread 'his' opus, which was written in a round and feminine hand. So that there would be no doubt of his authorship, he transcribed word by word the entire manuscript in a notebook on whose cover he wrote *The Vampyre: Preliminary Notes for a Tale*. The notebook turned into fifty pages of scribbles in a perfectly unintelligible hand, a shaky scrawl to which his tremor had contributed. Such was the conviction with which he worked that he ended up persuading himself of his own paternity of the manuscript. He made a number of opinionated corrections which he then crossed out with equal determination, only to be left with the original text.

After three days and three nights of hesitations and revisions, the final wording of *The Vampyre* did not differ in a single comma from the master draft. When all was finished, he made sure to destroy, without any remorse, the proof of his ignominy. Faithful to the example set by the real author, he devoured the whole bundle, page after page, literally allowing the word to become flesh.

VII

ON THE FOURTH DAY JOHN WILLIAM POLIDORI left his room. He was impeccably dressed. This was the stipulated night, when each member of the house party was to read out their promised tale, starting at the exact hour of midnight. From the landing, John Polidori saw that the hall had been especially set out for the event: four candelabra placed at the four corners of the room gave out a deathly light that barely reached the table. Through the large windows he could see a grey and cloudy sky which lent the occasion the air of a wake. Lord Byron and Percy Shelley were sitting at either end of the table, Mary and Claire on facing sides, each holding a manuscript. No one had noticed Polidori watching them from the darkness of the stairs. The truth is, no one expected the secretary to come to the rendezvous. It was some time before it dawned on Polidori that they had not even kept a place for him at the table. A burning indignation rose in his throat. But the recollection of the manuscript he carried under his arm was enough to calm him down: it wasn't worth his while to vent his anger on these poor conceited fools.

'I see you were not expecting me,' he said pleasantly, while descending the stairs with a mincing step.

Lord Byron, struck dumb, offered him his own seat. Polidori begged him not to trouble himself: he preferred to remain standing. That way, he thought, he would seem even more eloquent. Courtesy dictated that one of the two women should begin, but such was Polidori's excitement that, though no one had asked him to start, he took up his manuscript and began to read:

'*It happened that in the midst of the dissipations attendant upon a London winter, there appeared at the various parties of the leaders of the* ton *a nobleman, more remarkable for his singularities than his rank* . . .'

John Polidori read calmly, from time to time lifting his malicious gaze to settle it upon the astonished faces of his audience. Casting his eyes down again after staring pointedly at his lordship, he continued:

'*His peculiarities caused him to be invited to every house; all wished to see him, and those who had been accustomed to violent excitement, and now felt the weight of* ennui, *were pleased at having something in their presence capable of engaging their attention.*'

Walking round the table, the secretary read on. While he deliberately attempted to increase the impact of his words with meaningful looks, he noticed that his text was producing the desired effect: his audience was spellbound. And yet the allusions to present company were so subtle that, had one of them been seen to take offence, that person would have seemed utterly foolish.

'*Aubrey* (he read, looking Shelley straight in the eyes) *being put to bed was seized with a most violent fever, and was often delirious; in these intervals he would call upon Lord Ruthven* (fixing his eyes on Byron) *and upon Ianthe* (shifting his gaze to rest on Claire) – *by some unaccountable combination he seemed to beg his former companion to spare the being he loved . . .*'

Polidori continued to read without interruption, watched aghast by the others, until he reached the last words of his tale:

'. . . *Lord Ruthven had disappeared, and Aubrey's sister had glutted the thirst of a VAMPYRE!*'

Polidori put down his manuscript. There was a deathly silence full of fear, astonishment and respect.

'Very well, and now I am anxious to hear your own tales,' said the secretary.

Byron stood up, grabbed his few pages and threw them into the fire. Claire and Shelley did the same. Polidori attempted a gesture of studied distress. Mary, however, then opened her folder and prepared herself to read. As she was about to speak, John Polidori, deliberately seeking to give offence, disdainfully interrupted her:

'You must excuse me, I must be off to my room. I have important matters to attend to.'

As he was closing the door of his room, he thought he heard Mary utter the word 'Frankenstein'. He laughed heartily at his mistake.

VIII

JOHN WILLIAM POLIDORI WAS THE HAPPIEST
man in the world. He planned that, on his
return to London, the first thing he would do
would be to deliver the manuscript of *The
Vampyre* to Byron's own publisher: nothing could be more
humiliating for his lordship. But then he suddenly realized
that his tale, destined as it was to set a new style, was, in
spite of its genius and dark splendour, a bit slender to grant
him a passport to fame and glory. Looking at the small
bundle of not more than fifty pages, he told himself that a
single story, however sublime and new, was nothing compared, for instance, to his lordship's vast oeuvre. He could
already hear Byron's ironic comments on his secretary's
'complete works'. Polidori was overwhelmed by an anguish
deeper than the lake outside his window. Through the
curtain of water incessantly falling from the skies, he tried

to make out the small light on the faraway hilltop. But he saw nothing. In spite of his revulsion, he told himself that he would be willing to give anything for the sake of another book.

And so John Polidori anxiously awaited a sign from his collaborator. However, during the following three days, Annette Legrand failed to show herself; she had vanished with the same mysterious wilfulness with which she had first made herself known. John Polidori, thirsty for glory, was prepared to give up the last drop of his vital substance in exchange for new stories. Was it not true, as had often been said with a touch of hyperbole, that literary works are the children of their authors? Why then not agree that he was the father of those pages, since he had literally spent his seed in order to give life to each of those fictional characters? He was literally, not metaphorically, the true author of *The Vampyre* and now, willing to multiply and filled with paternal longings, he offered himself as the progenitor of new and sombre creatures of the word. This belief freed him from any feelings of guilt. Determined to climb to the very summit of celebrity, John Polidori reached the conclusion that if it was necessary to descend to the miserable hell of humiliation to achieve his purpose, he was prepared to do so. With the feverish resolution of a new Faust, he dipped his pen in the inkpot and began to write out a new contract.

I X

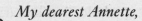*My dearest Annette,*
You are indeed the most horrible, revolting and ugly being that I have ever had the misfortune to meet. The description you gave me earlier of your person was kind compared to the truth of your appearance. And your soul does not lag far behind. However, I must admit that the story you bequeathed me is perfectly sublime. I don't know how you managed to delve into my spiritual self and uncover the most hidden, the most shameful and the darkest secrets of my being. No one can doubt the authorship of The Vampyre *because it never deviates from the story of my own life. You are like the devil himself, foul and terrible. But now I have a need of your talent just as you covet my seed. I am therefore prepared to enter willingly a secret marriage. Just as a*

noble lord requires female flesh to beget children and to prolong his proud line, I must have your continued company.

I will expect you this very night.

John Polidori left the letter next to the candlestick. He even had the grace to place upon it a white orchid.

JOHN POLIDORI WOKE UP EXCITED AS A CHILD. The first thing he did was look on his desk. Indeed, in the expected place by the candlestick, lay the new letter. He opened the envelope and, smiling innocently, began to read:

Dear Dr Polidori,
When you read this letter, I shall no longer be here. We
have decided to abandon Geneva for reasons upon which
I shall not dwell but which no doubt you can guess. You
can't know how honoured I am by your wedding pro-
posal. I must confess I never dreamt that someone would
offer me his hand and least of all a handsome young
man like you. I'm sorry I cannot comply with your
wishes. I loathe formal engagements. You men are never
satisfied with what you have. Be content with The

Vampyre *which, in all modesty, is far too good for a poor quack condemned to live in his lordship's shadow. You must accept this fact: you are good for nothing else. Even if you were to write books like those of the beautiful Percy Shelley, you would never cease to be the pauper son of a clerk, and if you ever became a father, you would sire only other miserable clerks such as yourself. Don't deceive yourself: you have no claim to aristocracy other than that which is granted to you by the shadow of Lord Byron. Furthermore, why do you suppose that your vital fluid (delicious as it is) is the only one at my disposal? Fortunately there are millions of men in this world. And paternity is always a matter of doubt.*

I am honoured by the epithets which you bestow upon me. But I would advise you, for the sake of your prose, to avoid overusing them. You called me a devil and I thank you for the compliment. But I must remind you that it is the devil who chooses the souls he wishes to buy and that he would never show interest in a miserable soul offered to him willingly.

Be satisfied with what I have given you. Farewell, my dear Pollydolly.

John Polidori had to sit down so as not to fall. He was used to being the victim of the most shameful humiliations. It was as if his very nature demanded always to be mortified, and yet he had never felt so despised. He wept inconsolably. In the mirror, he looked at his deplorable features and thought he saw reflected in them the traits of a dog, just like Boatswain, his lordship's Newfoundland. His destiny, he said to himself, resembled that of the miserable beast that trotted behind Lord Byron. Nevertheless, if he were to die then and there, he could certainly not expect a tomb like that which Byron had built for Boatswain at Newstead Abbey, and certainly not the epitaph he had written for his pet:

To mark a friend's remains these stones arise;
I never knew but one, – and here he lies.

John Polidori now wept like a dog, with long and disconsolate wails, and interminable howls.

Once again he was the sad secretary, the buffoon, the invisible phantom, the poet's scrivener, the failed doctor, the unknown Pollydolly.

John Polidori leaned against the window. It was raining furiously. He saw the darkness of Lake Leman, and his eyes were drawn once again towards the mountaintop. He thought he saw a faint light in the house that blended with the rocks on the peak. Suddenly, his face lit up. He ran downstairs with a demented look, crossed the hall, picked up one of the rifles that hung above the hearth, and bolted from the house. He splashed through the mud, soaking wet, falling, picking himself up again, crawling on all fours. Over his eyebrow, a trickle of blood was washed away by the rain only to spring up once more. His face was pink with blood and water. He ran desperately towards the lake. He reached the small pier. The planks creaked, lashed by the furious waves. The small boat rocked violently. Polidori had decided to murder the horrible three-headed monster. He pointed the rifle towards the opposite shore and, without aiming at anything in particular, he pulled the trigger. Then he threw the rifle into the water, to be rid of it, and jumped, blind with fury, into the boat. Polidori would never know that his shot had miraculously put out the flame of a distant candle.

Lake Leman foamed like an enraged animal. Polidori had to row against the current, but this didn't tire him in the slightest. Fuelled by wilful determination, he plunged the oars into the waves. He rowed with neither skill nor method. At his back, the mountaintop maliciously seemed to retreat further the harder he advanced.

Full of hatred and lashed by the rain, Polidori didn't notice that the water was lapping at his ankles. The boat had begun to sink. Like Charon crossing to his own hell, he rowed through the black waters that would have struck terror into the heart of the most experienced of sailors. The boat leapt from wave to wave, crashing against the walls of water, now sinking its prow, now rising and falling as if in flight. The oars flailed in the air. The boat rose, turned, and fell back keel upwards. A tongue of water held it in its grip and a second later the lake had devoured it. Polidori, however, had been thrown some distance from the boat. His north, his guiding star, was the light that shone with ever more intensity on the mountain peak. He swam without technique or method like a desperate beast, holding his head high above the water, abandoned to the furious course of the waves. He was guided by pure instinct; had he suddenly begun to think rationally, he would have been sure to drown.

Somehow John Polidori reached the opposite bank. Unaware of the extent of his own feat, he climbed up the moss-covered rocks, often losing his grip as he had lost his mind. He paid no attention to the fact that he had refuted his lordship's claim of superiority: swimming across a peaceful river was nothing compared to what he had just done. He reached the foot of the mountain. Between two rocks and beyond the black remains of a tree hit by lightning, began a tortuous path that crept up the slope. He didn't stop to catch his breath. He climbed with a firm step over the trail of boulders, bordered by funereal pine trees that bent in the wind. From where he stood, Polidori was not able to make out the peak, only the rocky slope down which ran furious streams of water, dragging along anything that stood in their way. On the other side was the abyss. Polidori had failed to notice that beyond the trees to his right fell a precipice whose depth was hidden by low clouds. The stones he dislodged while climbing rolled to the edge and fell into a fathomless darkness. The lake was now like a faraway ghostly field, a vast corpse lying under a winding sheet of mist. At last, Polidori had reached the mountaintop.

The light Polidori had seen from his room came from a tiny window; the house turned out to be a small and ancient castle built into the crags, a miniature acropolis carved in stone, overlooking the city of Geneva. Huge medieval doors hinged to the rock led to a sort of natural nave: Polidori pushed through them and found himself inside the enclosure. He closed the doors behind him. It took him some time to become used to the gloom and see where he was going. Feeling his way, he reached a chamber in which the wind blew even more fiercely than outside. As his eyes grew accustomed to the faint light, a desolate scene began to take shape: like a citadel ravaged by the plague, the chamber seemed to have been recently abandoned. Here and there he could see articles of female clothing, leftover food and papers that had not been entirely consumed by the embers in the hearth. A stench pervaded everything, a stench made up of various contradictory smells that seemed to come from different parts of the castle. Polidori singled out a particular odour. He followed its trace until he reached a bedroom: two identical beds covered in identical linens, above which hung two identical crucifixes. A pair of identical candlesticks with candles burnt down to the same level stood on two identical night-tables.

John Polidori left the room in search of the source of the

acrid odour. It was, he said to himself, like the nauseating smell from water closets or from the more sordid Greek whorehouses, a smell he thought he recognized in his own soiled trousers. He took a narrow corridor that soon became a flight of uneven steps. At the top was a small door. Without doubt, the unbearable smell came from the room behind that door. He had to bend down so as not to hit his head on the beam. The room was a minuscule cell, unsuitable even for an animal. Its only furnishings were a tiny straw bed and a diminutive desk set under the window. The remains of a candle were still burning. He approached the window and could see through it, on the other side of the lake, the whole of the Villa Diodati laid out before him and, in the very centre, the window of his own room. Under the desk was a small trunk. Polidori grabbed it by the handles and opened it avidly.

He saw hundreds of papers carefully ordered. The top one, he noticed, was his own letter, the one he had written the previous day. Beneath it was a booklet: the notes for *The Vampyre*. He pulled it out and underneath there appeared a thick bundle of corrrespondence. He immediately recognized the handwriting of the top letter, but he could not believe his eyes. When he read the signature, he almost died of shock. And he had not yet read its contents.

HE KNEW HIS LORDSHIP'S HANDWRITING better than his own. But what was a letter from Byron doing there, in the disgusting lair of the monster of whose existence only he, the unfortunate Polidori, was aware? The more he read and reread the heading, the less he understood, as if the round clear letters were incomprehensible characters, scribbled in an unknown tongue.

Abominable muse of darkness,
I have just finished reading the second part of your Manfred *(or should I say 'my'* Manfred*) and I must tell you that, if the first verses showed promise, these following ones were simply enthralling. They have a certain Byronesque tone which renders them exquisite. I trust you have fed to your heart's content (you cannot*

complain of the abundance of your last meal) and, judging by your literary production, my vital fluid seems to have filled you with my own splendid inspiration. The child Manfred has all the qualities of his noble father. I truly like him. If you continue in this fashion, I shall fall in love. I have no idea where your evil talent comes from, from where you have plucked Manfred's voice which, between the icy walls of his Gothic cathedral, sounds as dramatic and rootless as my own. His guilt, fathomless and irredeemable, is the forerunner of a guilt that I well know will torment me to my dying day. I need not tell you why. I have not read Faust *(I have no German) but, as luck would have it, some time ago my friend Matthew Lewis translated a long fragment[1] for me,* viva voce, *and I felt then under the very same spell conjured up now by my reading of* Manfred. *How I wish I were your hero and as resilient as he was in the face of temptation! But as you can see, I cannot even resist the temptation of claiming* Manfred *as my own.*

John Polidori felt the most foolish of men. He was overcome by a bitterness similar to that of a cuckolded husband. The only thought that comforted him was that his lordship, the magnificent poet, was as miserable a creature as himself.

[1] This fragment is almost identical to another that appears in one of Lord Byron's letters to Murray.

He rummaged through the papers in the stench-filled room until, losing all self-control, he plunged his hands wildly into the trunk and pulled out a handful, which he threw up into the air. One letter stuck to his sleeve, and he read it. It was written in French.

Notre Horrible Dame,

If it depended on my humble person, the ministry occupied today (or should I say 'usurped') by the ridiculous Count Rasumovski[2] *would be yours. His monstrous nature belongs to a typology far more abject than your own. The Minister can only wish for a talent such as yours, but I fear he has nothing to give you in exchange, since he lacks even the vigour of Fotij, our Archimandrite – 'Free us, O Lord, poor sinners, from such shepherds'*[3] *– who apparently shows equal passion for the souls of men and the bodies of women. With more reason than His Reverence, I can repeat the words he addressed to Madame Orlov: 'What have you done to me, turning my body into my soul?'*

I have read with great pleasure the second part of your Queen of Spades. *It is indeed something I wish I were writing myself. I very much want to know how 'my' story will end. I shall expect you tonight.*

Alexander Pushkin.

---

[2] Minister of Culture under Alexander I, to whom Pushkin addressed a fierce epigram.
[3] Beginning of the first of three epigrams addressed by Pushkin to the Archimandrite.

Among the letters there were hundreds of names unknown to him. Polidori felt an utter fool. Not only because he had been ignominiously duped, but because his competitors were unworthy scoundrels, lovers without fame or glory or future. He read the signatures as sadly as a lord cuckolded by his valet. Three letters were from a certain E. T. W. Hoffmann, half a dozen from someone called Ludwig Tieck. He pulled out more letters, hoping to find at least a few celebrated names, but all he found were more nobodies: Chateaubriand, the Duke of Rivas, a Spaniard called Fernán Caballero, and a certain Vicente López y Planes who prided 'himself' on having written the Argentinian national anthem.

He hunted at random through the innumerable letters in the trunk, blinded by hatred. He pulled out one last letter.

It carried the signature of Mary Shelley. Reading the first paragraph, he blanched. He had witnessed and taken part in all sorts of horrible events, but he had never read anything so bleak or so hellish. John Polidori was unable to go on. The words swam in front of his eyes and became meaningless shapes. He fainted.

Never again would John Polidori recover his reason, until the day of his premature death.

XII

 FEW ARE THE FACTS THAT HAVE COME DOWN to us regarding John Polidori's life in the four years after the fateful summer that changed the course of world literature. From his own journal, it becomes clear that the young doctor (who was, in Byron's words, 'more apt to induce illnesses than to cure them') was on an irrevocable path towards madness. Taking advantage of his lordship's absence, Polidori delivered to Byron's publisher the manuscript of *The Vampyre* in 1819. The tale was published and, contrary to Byron's own prediction, the entire print run sold out on the first day. The work, however, was published not under Polidori's name, but under Byron's. Indignant and furious, Byron wrote to the publisher from Venice a letter vehemently denying authorship. The misattribution was cemented by Mary Shelley: in the preface to her novel *Frankenstein*, in which she describes the circumstances under which she had conceived her creature in the rainy summer of 1816, in the Villa Diodati, she mentions the pact by which they had 'agreed to write each a story, founded on some supernatural occurrence'. Towards the end of the short preface, Mary Shelley falsely claims that 'the weather, however, suddenly became serene; and my two friends left me on a journey among the Alps, and lost, in the magnificent scenes which they present, all memory of their ghostly visions. The following tale is the only one which has been completed.' For some strange reason, the author of *Frankenstein* decided to omit an account of the birth of *The Vampyre* and to ignore, with the cruellest of silences, John William Polidori.

It was while he was on his Italian journey, during his sojourn in Pisa in 1821, that Byron was told of his secretary's suicide. He was deeply and sincerely affected. Perhaps it might have been of some consolation to him to know that the poor Pollydolly, without ever becoming conscious of it, had proved himself capable of the three feats Byron had listed as unachievable for him.

History has left sufficient proof of the Legrand twins' passage. In the books of the Hôtel d'Angleterre their names appear among those of the registered guests. However, it is very unlikely that the supposed third sister ever existed. I for one have not been able to obtain the slightest shred of evidence to that effect.

I am not willing to hold as proof the black envelope,

sealed with red wax, and in whose centre one can make out an almost illegible letter *L*, which appeared suddenly on my work desk and which I have not yet had the courage to open.